10/04

D0842823

Daughter of the Wind

Daughter of

Orchard Books / New York

An Imprint of Scholastic Inc.

A novel by

Michael Cadnum

the

Wind

Library of Congress Cataloging-in-Publication Data
Cadnum, Michael.
Daughter of the wind : a novel / Michael Cadnum.
p. cm.
Summary: In medieval times as various groups of Vikings fight for supremacy
of the northern lands and waters, Hallgerd, Gauk, and Hego, three young
people from the quiet coastal village of Spjothof, find their fates intertwined
as a series of events take them into danger far from home.
ISBN 0-439-35224-X
1. Vikings — Juvenile fiction.   [1. Vikings — Fiction.   2. Adventure and
adventurers — Fiction.   3. Coming of age — Fiction.   4. Middle Ages —
Fiction.]   I. Title.
PZ7.C11724 Dau 2003
[Fic] — dc21
2002072286

10   9   8   7   6   5   4   3   03   04   05   06   07

Printed in the U.S.A.   37
First Scholastic edition, August 2003

For Sherina

*Snow falling
into the sky*

One

There was a bear on the ice.

Gauk was pleased to see Snorri's signal that he had found tracks, waving and leaping up and down, pointing and making running motions with his arms so there could be no mistaking the message.

Gauk couldn't keep from laughing as he waved in return. But at the same time, the young hunter was suddenly thankful for the spear in his grip, aware that it was not too late to turn back to the boat, and to safety.

Gauk climbed to a ridge, his steps squeaking and crunching on the sun-weakened crust. He shielded his eyes and tried to see the creature. He could make out only ice and sky.

Snorri waved again. He was a bulky figure far across the immense floe, his leather cloak so stuffed with fleece that he looked like a much more heavyset man. Even at this distance Gauk could catch the flash of sunlight off Snorri's teeth as he smiled, gesturing excitedly, *Come look!*

Like most young Norsemen, both of them were trained at spear, sword, and knife. The two companions had hunted other large prey, even the bull walrus, on other spring days like this one. Walrus were great snorting, lunging creatures, exhaling geysers of vapor, and it took skill and a stout heart to kill one. But neither of the two young men had hunted bear before, and Gauk wondered once again how wise they were to take on this most dangerous quarry.

Their home village of Spjothof was famous as a proud place but poor, a village of brave men and beautiful women. But just a few weeks before, three warships, *Raven of the Waves, Crane,* and the legendary *Landwaster,* had returned laden with treasure from lands far to the west. The three ships had left again after a celebratory feast, eager to transform the newfound gold and silver into horses and sheep, and to spread the word of their success to villages up and down the fjord-cut coast.

Gauk and Snorri were proud of the three ships, but quietly chafed against their own lack of glory and wealth. Gauk had seen seventeen summers, and Snorri eighteen, and both felt spurred to win silver of their own. They had traveled here to the far north, past the taunts of pirates and drifting icebergs, hoping to track a bear on one of the vast floes. A

cub would earn good coin from a Frankish nobleman —
bears were prized in the fighting pits of the kingdoms of the
south. A bear too big to net and cage could be killed for its
valuable pelt. Such furs were prized because no land creature
was as big, or as fierce, as a bear, and there was no telling
how many hunters had died in its pursuit.

Before Gauk could reach his friend, a sky-splitting crack
rang out across the ice.

He stopped his progress across the crust, breathing hard.
Floes like this were liable to sudden fissures and sinkholes.
Even now the surface was trembling, and another report,
softer, like a cow's calving groan, filled the air.

Snorri waved him on, *Hurry!*

The reindeer-fur soles of his boots kept Gauk from slipping as he ran once again, clumsily fastening his garment.
By the time Gauk panted up to the icy hummock where
Snorri was waiting, his friend had given up his mocking
posture and was kneeling, examining a series of paw prints,
blue in the glittering surface.

They were huge.

Everyone knew the story of Egil the Stout — a yearling
bear had clawed him to death on the drift-ice some ten years
earlier, within sight of Egil's yelling, helpless companions. But
this was a mature bear, very large, heading steadily north.

"Does he know we're after him?" asked Snorri.

"He's in a hurry," answered Gauk, still breathing hard with exertion and excitement.

"He must be running from you," said Snorri with a laugh. "Gauk, the great hunter. He's heard of you."

Gauk laughed quietly, and sniffed the cold air. Was it his imagination, or could he smell bear-kill — seal flesh — somewhere on the ice?

Snorri put a hand to his own breast, whispering a prayer. He carried a little silver hammer in a pouch against his breast so Thor would bless their hunt. But Gauk suspected that the god most likely to lend support to an eager pair of hunters was Thor's father, the one-eyed Odin. The enigmatic god often took on the guise of such a great bear when he traveled the earth. Sometimes he rewarded an especially brave hunter with bear-spirit, giving the spearman a supernatural gift of fighting prowess.

Gauk breathed a silent prayer of his own. Only a short prayer — he wanted Odin's help, if he could spare it, but not his full attention. The wily divinity was known to speak to humans through animals. Gauk had never heard a beast talk, although he admired men like Thorsten, the village *berserkir,* a warrior who had been rewarded by Odin for some brave deed in the past.

To Gauk, such a man seemed the essence of manliness, and represented the freedom to engage in violent adventures. Not everyone admired such folk. Like many *berserkirs,* Thorsten was feared as a fighter, but not necessarily respected as a neighbor by householders and farmers. Berserkers lacked that essential element of self-control, so prized among the Norse.

Gauk had secret hopes of someday becoming a dreaded berserker himself, but he had not confessed this to anyone, even to Snorri. Gauk cared a great deal what his neighbors thought of him, and he was not sure that the power to annihilate opponents was worth the sideways glances a berserker received.

Besides, thought the young hunter, if Odin ever spoke to me in the guise of a bear, I would die of fright.

"How fresh are the tracks?" Snorri was asking, fingering the cub net tied to his hip, useless against an adult bear. Perhaps Snorri, too, was having second thoughts, and beginning to hope that this bear-spoor was not recent.

"Very fresh," replied Gauk, trying to disguise the strain in his voice, and the two friends laughed at their own nervousness.

"Do you think he'll turn and come back?" asked Snorri, careful to face away from the gentle north wind so his speech would not carry. Gauk had a reputation for foretelling weather and judging where the submerged whale would surface. He had a strong arm, too, and older men let

Gauk make the first harpoon thrust when a bull walrus charged across the ice.

Gauk considered. He had heard the saga masters, fueled by ale, sing of bear hunts, and he had seen the scars of the sun-darkened men who had tried cub-snatching, and given it up.

"Maybe," Gauk guessed, his voice a bare whisper, "when he reaches the edge of the ice, he'll turn around and test us."

The animal's tracks were deep — he was traveling fast, into the eye of the wind — but bears were, by reputation, much like men: restless, proud, and curious. And however vast the floe might be, the island of ice did not stretch forever.

It was not too late for the two hunters to change their minds — a short walk south and they would reach their *skip,* the small sailing boat, shake out the white, homespun sail, and begin the long voyage home.

Then Gauk felt ashamed of himself, aware that he was demonstrating a lack of true courage. Snorri wanted a bear, and Gauk could not blame his friend for his ambition or high spirits.

Everyone could recite the brief saga of Atli, a legendary fighter, who tracked a she-bear three days and three nights, until he roared out "The Tracker's Challenge." This was one of the Spjotfolks' favorite songs, one that inspired hunters to greater endurance and charmed prey into helplessness. The bear responded to the song somewhat unexpectedly, turned around, and chased Atli all the way to his ship. The story was considered amusing, but in every important respect true.

"If he comes back to take a look at us —" Snorri made a plunging motion with his spear, as though the kill would be as easy and natural as breaking flatbread and passing it around. They had heard the gray-haired hunters describe how two hunters, with paired, angled thrusts, were more likely to slay a bear. Four hunters would do even better — or eight.

Gauk could not shake off his dread.

The thunder from below startled both of them. Snorri made an expression of exaggerated fear as the great floe rocked underfoot, but Gauk could not laugh.

The ice was breaking up, frost-smoke rising up in the distance.

The floe trembled for what seemed a long time.

Snorri stopped sporting and leaned on his spear, using it as a staff. The ice desert shivered underfoot once more, and then at last it was still.

"Calm down," said Snorri, speaking to the frozen surface around them. He knelt and gave the glittering crust a pat. "You nearly frightened poor Gauk." His voice was steady but husky, his fear badly disguised.

"I can swim better than you can," said Gauk, for the moment slightly resenting his friend's ability to turn everything into an attempt at humor. Gauk could name several hunters who had disappeared through rotten ice in the history of their village, or who had vanished into a sudden ice-fog never to be seen again. Gauk could swim, after a fashion, but the cold water would kill any man in very little time.

Snorri began to chant, as loudly as he could.

He recited the ancient challenge.

> *Redden no more*
> *the ice with your tread —*
> *weary creature, come home to my spear.*

The soul-stirring tune was lost in the cold air. The chant reminded Gauk so much of long nights around the ale fire, voices joined in poetry, that he was silenced by a stab of longing for home.

Gauk joined in, their two voices strong, now, warming to the song.

Two

♦ ♦ ♦

They fell silent at the end of the ancestral chant.

The two friends shielded their eyes against the ice loom —
the glare of the white surface reflected in the sky — searching
the horizon.

"See anything?" asked Snorri.

Gauk, whose eyes were admired for their acuity, did not respond. He did not want to give voice to disappointing news.

Gauk's father had been lost in a storm at sea three summers past. Sometimes Gauk wondered what his father would
advise him at a time like this. *Go back,* he would no doubt
counsel his son, *and let some other father's son lose his life.*

Gauk hoped that Astrid would be watching on the shore
when he and Snorri rowed the still waters of the fjord, with
a huge snowy pelt in the prow of the boat. Astrid was as
pretty as Hallgerd, the jarl's daughter, but more likely to
laugh at a young hunter's joke, or walk with him to the edge
of the sheep meadow. Gauk had woven her a bracelet of

straw during the long winter darkness, a cunning piece of work. Astrid had blushed with pleasure on receiving it from his hand.

"Is he on his way?" Snorri was asking.

No seemed too final.

"Not yet," said Gauk. "I'm sure he liked my singing very well, but yours —"

Snorri gave a quiet, disappointed laugh. The young hunter used his sleeve as a strop, whetting his iron spearhead. Whale-Biter had been found by Snorri's mother in a whalebone washed up in the fjord. Hego, the village's master at putting an edge on iron, had taken special care, honing the storied spear. Gauk's own spear was a good enough weapon, but without a name. Only soul-stirring events or an intriguing history could make a weapon, or any object, name-worthy.

Gauk put a finger to his lips, and Snorri crouched expectantly.

Gauk separated from his friend and took several strides, climbing a high mound. He shaded his eyes against the afternoon sun. A gust of wind made him blink, tears blurring his vision.

Nothing moving.

Nothing there.

And yet Gauk told himself to look with his entire body, with his memory and his love of life. To see what was there, even if his eyes could not yet make it out.

Gauk blinked twice, just to be sure.

He gave a low, sharp whistle. "He's bigger than I thought," he said. *Much bigger than the creature whose hide hangs in the jarl's house,* he could not add in his excitement. "And he's on his way here."

"How far away?" asked Snorri.

He was closer than Gauk expected, and coming on much too quickly.

Then, without warning, the bear vanished.

It was an old hunter's adage: When a bear goes to ground, keeping his black snout behind the ridges, he becomes invisible.

Gauk said, "He's stalking us." His pulse hammered.

And before the young hunter could add anything more, the ice groaned again, making a noise like a mare in heat, like a whole herd of randy steeds. The spine of snow under his feet shifted, forcing him to sink to one knee. With slow thunder, a long abyss worked its way across the ice, exhaling cold.

When the ice fell silent, a crevasse separated the two friends.

*　*　*

Snorri tiptoed to the edge, a daring demonstration of how close he could get, crumbs of ice crust tumbling into the darkness. He shook the net at his hip. He acted it out, the throw, the hauling, Gauk rejoining his friend on the north side of the crevasse.

Could the net, and Snorri's strength, support Gauk's weight?

Gauk was broad-shouldered and tall, but surely his friend would have little trouble. Very little trouble. And yet the young man's habitual caution flickered to life. A better plan was to walk along the abyss, searching for an ice bridge. Such cracks did not run forever.

The void was a source of wind, now, and it would be hard to make himself heard over the breathy echo, the depths still resounding with the rupture in the floe.

And as the echo subsided, there was another sound.

A quiet sound, growing louder, closer. Gauk realized too late what this new disquiet was, this ponderous *chuff, chuff* growing more distinct across the wind-carved snow.

The beast was closing fast.

And Snorri did not see him.

Three

Gauk did not have to cry out a warning.

Even at this distance his friend read it in his eyes.

Snorri spun, and danced away from the crevasse. He half-crouched, his spear poised, and skipped backward, nimble and well balanced. The bear was traveling with too much momentum to alter his course, and for an instant Gauk had a vision of the great animal tumbling into the abyss.

Each bound the bear made cast a ripple of yellow-white fur in a wave over his body and caused a burst of air to escape his nostrils. He struggled to brake his course, his paws skidding over the gleaming surface. Snorri scampered up a ridge of ice and turned to face the bear as the animal altered his approach, explosions of white vapor where he had been an instant before.

Gauk cried out.

The bear slowed, gathering himself. He swung his paws,

sluggish, weighed down with his expanse of seal-stained fur. Neither blow struck Snorri, who fell to his knees.

The bear is bluffing, Gauk tried to reassure himself. He's got a belly full of seal, and will soon tire of the two of us. And Snorri is clever. Gauk ran along the crevasse to keep what was happening in full sight as his friend Snorri fell, rolled into a ball, and did not move.

Gauk began to leap along the edge of the crevasse, and lifted his shaking voice in a song, a village battle cry, *"Let not your breath touch my shipmate."* The bear turned, his small, iron eyes picking out Gauk where the young hunter danced at the far edge of the chasm.

Snorri rose and brandished his spear, whether to reassure Gauk that he was still alive, or to implore the powers of the sky, Gauk could not tell. His friend had been injured, after all, a rill of blood coursing down his face. But it was not a mortal wound, Gauk fought to believe. It was the sort of injury a man will live to brag about, running a finger along an old scar.

The massive bear turned and sniffed the air in Snorri's direction, as though he had trouble seeing the hunter. Then he drew close to Snorri, enveloping him in shadow.

"Now!" Gauk cried out. Or perhaps he prayed the words silently, sent them like Odin's sacred ravens to his friend's soul, *Now.*

Into his heart with the spear.

Gauk did not see the bear strike another blow. Or perhaps he saw it and his mind would not believe what it perceived. In an instant Snorri was not standing. He was stretched out on the ice.

The bear knelt over Snorri in a posture nearly maternal, protective, seeking the wound, licking, lapping, reaching down with his ever-reddening muzzle and working at Snorri. The creature shook his head back and forth. Bones broke, a subtle, heartrending whisper. Even at this distance Snorri's breath came out loud but wordlessly, and then all Gauk could see of his friend was a hand, extended from its sleeve, whipping back and forth across the widening red puddle on the snow.

Gauk leaped across the chasm. He plunged the spear into the ice, his caribou-fur mittens digging, finding a grip on the frozen ledge. But as he levered his body upward the spear tumbled, vanishing into the abyss, echoes rising up out of the cold. Gauk was weaponless.

He clung, his fingers slipping. He was bellowing, calling with all his power to distract the bear, to wake the beast from his intent, meditative occupation, like a pensive weaver worrying a knot.

Gauk flung one leg over the edge of the ice, slipped, and fought forward, onto the opposite side. He swung to his feet and crouched like a wrestler, poised, challenging. He beckoned to the bear. The animal turned from his work, and his tiny eyes took in the sight of the young hunter, looked away, and then looked back again.

The bear had an old walrus tusk wound on one shoulder, a hairless crescent. His teeth were amber yellow, his claws dark, paws bloodstained. The bear rounded away dismissively, bending over what had been Snorri.

Gauk had heard of fighting folk going down under the tide of an enemy with a song on their lips, and he had never quite believed it. Saga lore was woven of such imaginative touches. But now Gauk knew that there was such a chant — the one he was calling now, rich with grief for his friend, and freed from any hope for his own safety.

"Take me!" Gauk was crying, if any words could be shaped from such a wail. "Kill me, and leave my friend alone," he sang out.

Snorri's spear had spun far from the lake of blood. Gauk calculated quickly how many strides it would take to reach the weapon and, before he let himself entertain any further doubt, he leaped scrambling, reaching out for Whale-Biter.

The great creature made a rippling, hulking leap. The bear knocked Gauk down with the onrushing course of his attack, a lunge so powerful that the beast overshot the young hunter. Gauk had time to climb to his knees, but he was too badly shaken to stand.

The bear gathered himself and circled, his lower jaw hanging, wet and dark. The great animal hulked over Gauk, forcing the hunter down with his huge, square head, his breath smelling of ripe seal and fish and something else — the warm, kettle-broth odor of blood.

Gauk struck the beast with his bare fist, hard, on the snout.

The bear leaned back on his haunches, seeming to smile with his black lips, his gray tongue protruding.

"Me!" Gauk heard his voice cry.

"Kill me instead."

The bear lowered his snout, and Gauk gripped the bear's fur just below the animal's tiny ears. Gauk's hands, although big enough to gather ells of woven wool, and strong enough to wrestle a full-grown ram, were puny on either side of the wet-spiked head.

"Odin, hear me," sang Gauk in a half-whisper.

The bear exhaled, a long, moist wind.

And it seemed to Gauk a voice within his soul spoke, a bear's growl.

Pronouncing his name.

Four

Hego heard footsteps.

They woke him.

He lay there awake, listening to the gentle *lap-lap* of water in the fjord, and the silence of his beloved village of Spjothof.

Even the deepest water rises and falls gently, with a quiet more beautiful than perfect silence. No ship could steal along the fjord without disturbing the water, and waking the village long before the keel touched the gravel bottom. No intruder could approach along the beach without even his tiptoed progress crunching loudly in the pebbly ridges along the water. The land approach to the village was all high mountain, and no one but supernatural beings dwelled up so high, in the snowfields that never melted.

So, Hego reasoned, he was mistaken.

And yet.

He heard them again. Just two footsteps, out where feet

did not belong, on the high sheep meadows uphill from the village. One footstep, treading with a man's full weight. And then another just afterward, hurried, kicking a spray of field grass. Two different men.

Hego sat up. What would wanderers be doing so high above the village in the short summer darkness? Hego groaned as he fumbled for the water scoop. Earlier that summer he had fallen on his face, and the injury had prevented him from traveling on the newly launched *Raven* when the ship had voyaged for the west-land with the two other famous ships, *Landwaster* and *Crane*.

Even now, the three ships having come home in triumph, and then voyaging forth again to purchase flocks and barley up and down the coast, Hego had not been asked to join in. The young man was treated with affection, but no one considered him the equal of experienced warriors.

Hego drank cold water from the bucket beside his bedding, the water pleasingly flavored by the birch wood slats of the container. It was not enough. He was as thirsty as a man who had sweated three hours in a bathhouse, as thirsty as a man who had dined on an entire basket of salt cod. He climbed up from his pallet in the straw-littered corner of his cottage. His shop bench was a crowd of blades village folk had left for him to sharpen, scythes and fodder knives.

As he rose Hego was careful not to wake up Jofridr, the

serving woman who boiled his pork and whose thimble was kept busy mending his homespun.

Jofridr's snores stopped as he took a step, the dried rushes on the floor whispering.

"Rurik?" she inquired sleepily.

"I'm getting a drink of well water," said Hego gently.

Rurik was a helmsman lost in an ice storm many long winters ago, after less than a year of marriage to Jofridr.

Her deep, steady breathing started in again. She had served Hego's family for many years. When Hego's parents had died, not many winters ago, she had mourned them almost as deeply as Hego.

The young man took his battle-ax from the corner. Head-Splitter was a weapon equal to any in the village. At least, that was its reputation. Hego had never hurt anyone with it.

He stepped out under the night sky.

A mare heard his step and nickered, and Hego made a comforting, horse-like sound right back at her. He made out the grunt of Inga's flatulent breeding boar, and Old Gizzur Quickhand's deep, ponderous snoring, even though the skilled sheepshearer lived all the way at the edge of the village. Something about the night troubled Hego. He could not keep from wishing that hale Ulf were here, and lively Lidsmod, fighters with strong arms and good cheer, who could meet any foe.

Hego's head throbbed. Jofridr's ale was thick and power-ful, unlike the weak stuff brewed by other housekeepers. Ale drinking was a serious undertaking in Spjothof. A strong man was expected to be able to drink deeply and tell proud stories — how many seal skins he had brought back last summer, which comely woman was round with child be-cause of his prowess behind the ale hall. Hego could drink more fermented beverage than any man, winning every *kappdrykkfa* — drinking contest — during which horns of ale or rare mead were drunk without restraint. While the young man was a drinker of legend, to his shame he had no great reputation as a storyteller.

Hego listened hard, and he heard no more footsteps.

And then he did, once more, and the creak of leather. Heavy billy goat leather, or even ox leather, the sort men used for armor.

But this wasn't possible. Most of Spjothof's fighting men had sailed off again, and even old Hrof, a legendary, gray-haired fighter fond of wandering around in full-leather ar-mor, would not be walking around in the mountain passes at night.

Hego was slow, in both mind and body. He knew this,

hated himself for it, and sought to think faster at every opportunity. If some young men could grow more fleet of foot through practice running from the well to the shipyard, then Hego could learn to think more quickly.

It would take practice.

Not that Hego was utterly without skill. Children brought him their first knives, the short blades fathers gave their sons so they could learn the art of carving, a prized craft in the village. A good edge was highly honored in the village. Old men whittled mustached sea lords from the leg bones of deer, and children made their own, crude figures out of driftwood. It was an industry Spjothof was renowned for, carving elk antlers into spoons, cow bones into combs. Travelers docked here every summer to collect the fine reindeer-bone thread-spindles and whalebone sword pommels.

Now there was something wrong. The mare shook her mane, and scuffed the earth with one hoof. Some intruding presence was disturbing the livestock, there could be no question.

Hego sometimes walked out to the stone-lined water source just to listen to the wind make a whole, round song as it blew over the round opening in the earth. Now he lowered the bucket carefully. It did not have to descend far, the earth so full of water that Njord the helmsman had bet

Hego the well would overflow before *Raven* and its companion ships came home.

Another step.

Creeping, but distinct, and the *chink* of expensive metal armor.

Hego heard them clearly now, many men, far off across the snowmelt-sodden pasture. He counted them, as every Spjotman had been taught, numbering his unseen foe. Leather belts and booted feet, far off. And whispering voices. He could almost make out the words.

Hego walked out into the field grass and made a clicking sound with his tongue, the sort of quiet noise the hawk owl makes to its young. It was the traditional signal Spjotfolk gave to one other in the dark.

There was no response.

Hego smiled, despite his unease. This was when he would win his glory, fighting off an army of dwarves, the squat, earth-dwelling creatures who populated every song but never approached human dwellings. Now he would have a story. *Head-Splitter and I strode out under the stars,* he would say —

He stopped.

He heard the whirring sound, and a mutter of human speech, guessed who this enemy was as Head-Splitter — a breath-keen weapon that had never touched a scalp — roused, like a living thing.

These were not dwarves.

These were Danes!

Danes were legendary in Spjothof as wealthy and well armored, but fastidious in battle, preferring sling stones and arrows to hand-to-hand combat. A Danish voice whispered again, and another stone hummed through the air.

As yet another stone hissed past, and another, Hego readied his warning cry. Perhaps he would sing out, *The Danes have crept out of the mountain,* or, even better, *I'm killing Danes at the edge of the sheep meadow!*

He would say something grand, words villagers would repeat in ale halls up and down the coast, long after his bones were green earth.

But before Hego could make a single sound, a stone sang off the side of his skull.

And he knew nothing.

Five

The fire started in the hours before dawn.

Hallgerd heard it in her sleep, the sputter of far-off flames, and the airy roar as the timbers of the great hall began to blaze. In her half-dream the jarl's daughter thought it was the sound of wind, or a rough surf.

She woke.

The ruddy gleam of distant firelight worked under the cracks of the shuttered window. For an instant she thought the village fighting men must have all returned from voyaging, having loaded freight ships with grain and horses. They were all dancing around a great fire, her beloved Lidsmod among them.

She flung open her shutters. Her father's house was one of the few in the village with windows, three of them. As noble leader of the town, a jarl's dwelling was often distinctive. Hallgerd was proud of these openings in the timbered walls, and always hoped that her neighbors would observe her leaning out and enjoying the view. Now, as the predawn chill breathed into the house, she was certain she heard the crackling of fire overhead, too, on the roof of her family dwelling.

She cocked her head and heard nothing more, only the distant shouts of neighbors, spreading the alarm that the alehouse was alight. Some errant whisper caught her further attention, a sound from above. It was possible for someone to hide on a longhouse roof — the wooden eaves and occasional turf coverings easily camouflaged a leather-clad figure. People still told the story of Egil the Stout hoisting himself on a roof to surprise his wife, and falling asleep. A raven had awakened him, one of Odin's sly, sacred birds perching on his forehead, and people still chuckled over the great hunter's embarrassment.

But the roof above her made no further creak. Already figures were racing to the burning hall, veteran sailors and sheepmen, all of them accustomed to shipboard crises and sudden bad weather. Birch wood buckets already splashed from hand to fire, men and women stumbling from their dwellings, hurrying toward the great hall.

Her father put a hand on her shoulder in the half-dark of the longhouse and said, "Help Astrid with the ewes."

*   *   *

Hallgerd fastened her cloak as she ran, pinning it at one shoulder with the amber clasp that had belonged to her grandmother.

A pen full of bawling sheep struggled, kicking and jumping in the darkness. The creatures were so close to the blaze that the firelight danced in their panicked eyes. Livestock were often held in one common pen in the village. It pleased Hallgerd to consider that soon, thanks to riches won by the three fighting ships, freight-knorrs — heavy-timbered cargo vessels — would arrive with new breeding ewes, fatter and healthier than these tough, long-legged sheep.

Hallgerd had been trained to be proud of her family — but not too proud to attend livestock. She could lance a boil on a sow and keep a gander from biting by hissing right back at him, but she knew that a noble young woman of seventeen was expected to display a degree of dignity, clapping her hands to drive the sheep uphill through the village rather than kicking them and bawling like her friend Astrid, or whooping like the young boys who joined them.

Hallgerd used the low, steadying tone her mother had taught her, a no-nonsense sound the sheep responded to as they streamed through the village longhouses. The small herd flowed up into the dark meadow beyond as sparks from the fire descended all around them through the darkness.

Hallgerd caught the scent of the blaze, and turned.

As the flames consumed the seasoned spruce and pine the conflagration did not smell right. Fire was an endemic danger in such a timbered village, and stories were told of entire wooden towns burning, every roof down to every threshold, because of an errant spark.

A few gray-bearded men were hurrying back to their cottages and returning, strapping on swords. Hallgerd had been warned since childhood: Young women were a favorite battle-treasure, and some ships sailed simply to seek out a promising wife. The village of a stolen bride was often compensated with treasure, and marriage reduced to a rough sport benefiting everyone but the bride and any hometown suitor. Political alliances were sometimes forged through such bride-theft — even the loss of a daughter could be soothed with an offering of peace and wealth. Nevertheless, every family dreaded such a raid. *If an enemy breaks our ground with his booted foot,* her father had always cautioned her, using the language of the sagas, *arm yourself and stay within our home.*

Hallgerd and Astrid left the bawling, surging flock with shrill-voiced boys, and the two of them found the jarl. Hallgerd's father strode through the excited villagers, searching, reaching for her as he spied her at last.

"Go back to the house," Rognvald said, "and bolt the

shutters." He caught her arm gently, but with unmistakable urgency. "No one will make my daughter a battle-prize."

"Are we under attack?" Hallgerd asked breathlessly.

"I fear so," was all he would allow himself to say.

Hallgerd tried to suppress the fear that swept her just then. The jarl's daughter reminded herself again that women were frequently war booty, and that there were legendary sea warriors who simply seized women and carried them off, never to be seen again.

All the other young women were returning to their long-houses, too, Astrid hurrying off to her own dwelling near the shipyard. Sigrid, Hallgerd's mother, carried a spear, and looked more than capable, weapon in hand. The sagas were filled with tales of women who had battled intruders over the wounded bodies of their men.

Mother and daughter hurried back uphill, toward their home. The fire was too bright, Hallgerd knew, and it burned too fast. She had smelled it already, the cloying, fleshy smell of mink-whale oil, used to fuel the blaze.

The fire was a ruse, a threatening distraction. When old Gizzur Quickhand hurried from the edge of the village, sword in his grip, Hallgerd was not surprised to hear him call out, "Nightwalkers! Out in the high meadows!"

Sigrid put a hand on the old sheepman's tunic. "How

many?" she asked, the only question that mattered, whether the enemy was man or troll.

"Oh, Lady Sigrid," gasped Gizzur, unable for the moment to say more. He held up a hand, opening and shutting it, the time-honored way of signaling quantity from ship to ship, *five, ten, fifteen.*

Nightwalkers were the stuff of nightmares. Children woke screaming that shadowy, muscular night-men were stealing through the windows, down from the mountainside. No sane or reliable human went out wandering the night.

"Many," panted Gizzur.

"Are they Danes?" asked Sigrid.

Gizzur had traded livestock as far south as the Danish coast, but he could only say, "My eyes, good Sigrid —"

Are not what they used to be, was the unspoken apology.

Hallgerd wished that her father were beside them, but Rognvald was far off now, his voice lifted, giving orders. Hallgerd knew that her father enjoyed carrying out his duties as jarl. He was a wise man, and he valued this quality in himself. Leading his villagers in a fight against a blaze was the sort of deed the gods had created him to do, and he did it well.

The Danes were bitter, all the sea traders reported, for the raids some five summers earlier, waged by Spjothof's great ship *Landwaster.* The Spjotmen had attacked villages belonging to Halfdan the Bald and Spear-Harald, both jarls of high repute. Only the approach of ships belonging to Gudmund the Fair had sent the Spjotmen into retreat.

Gudmund was renowned for his sea-fighting prowess, although wise Spjotmen offered the opinion that he was less capable when he fought on land. This was, they explained, why the sea jarl had never sought out Spjothof in the years since. Spjotmen were renowned land-fighters, and the village was reputedly sacred to the Hammer God himself.

And unlike the easy-living villages to the south, the folk of Spjothof enjoyed plain fare. They rarely ate yeast bread, almost never drank cow's milk, and used their barley harvest strictly for the brewing of ale. Hallgerd knew there was nothing in Spjothof worth stealing, beyond pigs and sheep.

"Find Hego," Sigrid was telling Gizzur. "He has a dog's good sense."

And, she did not have to add, the young man had a strong arm and a serviceable ax. "Find him, drunk or sober, and put a weapon in his hands," Sigrid continued. "And stir the shipwrights and tell them to arm themselves and guard the mountainside approach."

"I'll go, too," said Hallgerd hopefully.

Sigrid gave a laugh.

"I can fight," Hallgerd insisted, "as well as any keel-shaver."

"And so can I," said her mother.

She did not have to add, *It isn't worth the risk.*

Six

In a wealthy village the jarl's house would be attended by many servants, the place ordered by an efficient *matselja* — housekeeper — with an obedient staff, all of them subservient to the master's wife. There might even be *thralls* — slaves — to grind barley ale and shift the heavy loads.

Here there was only Grettir, a woman heavily muscled from years of pounding salt cod with a mallet. She and Hrolf, a solidly built house guard, were all the household servants the jarl's family could afford, but they were two saga-worthy retainers. Grettir knew all the old rhymes, which charms kept away mice, and which ones soothed Freya the goddess of the earth.

"No one across this threshold but a friend," said Grettir, brandishing a meat cleaver.

Hrolf was missing three fingers on his shield hand from a legendary sword fight. A giant from Namdall bet him a purse of silver he could not last an hour fighting hand-to-hand. That had been long ago, before Hallgerd's birth, on a glorious midsummer feast night people still sang about. Hrolf's shield was cleft by a battle-ax, and had been followed by three other shields in succession, but the giant — the stoutest and tallest man anyone had ever seen — had at last suffered a heart attack and died.

"No wee little intruder is going to tickle any of the jarl's folk with the point of a knife," said the old warrior, for whom every subsequent opponent had been small. Hrolf straddled the doorway, and it was as though Thor himself straddled the door sill against intruders.

In one corner of the longhouse was the vast bear pelt, killed by the berserker Thorsten years before. Berserkers were troublesome, unpredictable men, but Hallgerd knew that one berserker could take on scores of ordinary fighters. Thorsten, like so many others, was voyaging now. Even the two young hunters, Snorri and Gauk, were away from the village. The two friendly, keen-eyed young men would have been beyond value on such a night.

"It's just like the Danes," said Sigrid, plucking the key ring from the wall, "to set the ale hall alight and plunder the cottages when the villagers go running."

It was a Spjothof trick, too, but Hallgerd did not want to point this out. It was the time-honored ruse any attacker used when he wanted to sack a village and avoid a battle.

Spjothof had never been attacked, throughout the generations, but this was an era when seafaring men sought out far-flung adventures.

The jarl's house was called Sword-Rest, both because of the jarl's reputation as a peacekeeper, and for its storage room of ancient and excellent weapons. The large longhouse was unusual among dwellings in that, in addition to a rush-strewn, pleasantly scented meeting and dwelling space, it had several storage rooms, including a *matbur* — a pantry, for the storage of food — and a *gervibur* — a weapons room.

A storage room was generally considered a woman's domain, and most men would have felt out of place in a curd room, or in a *suthrbur* — a south-room, where wort fermented into ale. Storage rooms were secured by heavy bronze padlocks, and opened with large, well-worn keys. Only the jarl himself generally entered the place where weapons were stored. Her mother had never, in Hallgerd's memory, set a key within its lock.

She flung the door wide.

Hallgerd's heart quickened. She was frightened, but it was a thrilling, joy-sweetened fear. Until she saw her mother remove the legendary Quern-Biter, her father's blade, from the weapons room, Hallgerd did not quite believe the danger of attack was real.

"Hold this sword," said her mother.

Hallgerd had been taught by her father how to swing a blade, but not one this heavy or so bright with legend. The sword was offered not only for its usefulness in combat, but for companionship. This had been the sword Hallgerd's grandfather had used to cut a millstone in two — or so the song went. He won a silver arm-ring on a bet, according to the story, and ever since, the steel was kept sweet with oil, but never used.

Sword in hand, ran the Saga of the Warrior Virgins, *no man can take me.*

Many of the houses had been built over diverted streams that sang under the flooring, to wash away the bodily soils and refuse of the households. There was water in plenty in this summer predawn, and already the fire was steaming, dying as Hallgerd leaned on the open window of her father's house, her grandfather's sword leaning on the wall beside her.

But the fire was anything but defeated. As the seething blanket of flames on the peaked roof was doused, trampled, beaten down by the villagers, a host of new flames erupted under another eave. The village still boasted enough sturdy men and women to put out a random fire. And that's all this was, Hallgerd was convinced now — a dwarfish blaze. Many sprites and powers hid even among human dwelling places, waiting to spill an ember from its place of safekeeping.

Once again Hallgerd heard a whisper from above, on the roof of her father's house. Her bedding place was far from the other living space of the longhouse, far from the hearth in the center of the floor, where the kettles hung and the ember pot kept its glowing spark all night. Her mother consulted with Hrolf in the doorway, heads together, and even from here Hallgerd could make out the beginning of a fire tale, a story of burning ships and singed aprons, a recounting of the many freak blazes the village had known, all of them smothered, each fire put to rest.

Hallgerd straightened her bedding in the far corner of the house, and — she would blush to remember this later — took off her hurriedly donned cloak and stripped to her linen underclothes, made from flax her father had bargained for with traders from far-off lowlands.

She left the sword in the corner, against the wall.

She pulled on clothing as a warm, predawn wind spilled through the open window. Soon all the villagers would gather to pick through the still-grand ruin of the ale hall, and the joiner and his apprentice would chop down green pines to replace the charred remains. Hallgerd would join them, all the villagers gathering to mourn the old hall, and begin the work of building it again.

As she folded her blanket of lamb's wool, she felt the presence before she saw it, the scent of goat leather and the creak of belt and buckle. A strong arm seized her, a hand clapped over her mouth.

She struggled and tried to call out, but she could make no sound.

A man's voice breathed into her ear, a hoarse whisper with a Danish accent, "Be silent, Hallgerd, or I'll cut off your nose."

The point of a blade pressed against her cheek.

Seven

Hallgerd tried to cry out again, but the sound was trapped by the callused hand over her mouth.

Hrolf and Grettir were in the hall beyond her bedchamber, so close that surely they would hear her squeal. Her mother was complaining that the door to one of the window shutters was warped and wouldn't close, and Hrolf was saying, "Let me shut it for you," his voice a study in dutiful solemnity.

Hallgerd made a noise through her nose. Her mother seemed to hear something, stopping midsentence.

Sigrid was listening, her attention a palpable presence. And then she started talking again.

Hallgerd snorted, wrestling, trapped in the arms that held her.

She struggled hard, kicking over a stool, striking the clothes chest as she swung her foot, digging her elbows sharply into her captor's sturdy body. As strong arms grappled with her, the sounds of swords clashing came from the darkness beyond, at the village edge.

Her wrists were bound together, and a gag was thrust into her mouth. A cloth sack was flung over Hallgerd's head. Even as she struggled, kicking, crying out against the salt-cured leather between her teeth, she was lifted like a bundle and handed out through the window.

She made as much noise as she could, stifled cries that must have been audible to any neighbor paying the smallest bit of attention. She dug the point of her chin, muffled within its sack, into the muscular back that bore her. The man grunted, but neither cursed her nor made any attempt to hurt her, aside from increasing his grip around her ankles.

You will eat my father's sword.

The man kept a steady loping stride, running with little sound over the soft pasture.

Ravens will prick your eyes.

She prayed to Odin the Cunning. She prayed to Thor, friend to plowman and woodgatherer. She prayed to her dead ancestors, the legendary Inga Alfsdottir, who invented the loom, and Ketill, who discovered the hot springs above Midwife Mountain. She prayed to gods of field and water, cursing this stranger.

Whoever carried her was traveling ever faster now, his shoulder forcing the breath from her body as she hung, head down, wrestling and wrenching from side to side. Blind within her wool sack, trying to guess the direction they were traveling, she was certain that at any moment her mother would cry out — or perhaps Hrolf, who had always been vain regarding his own watchfulness, would sound a warning.

Certainly her father would see what was happening, or a neighbor. And people did notice — she could hear the startled voices, but too late, too far behind — Grettir's cry, and Hrolf's, "She's gone!"

She could make out Rognvald's voice, "Men and women to their swords!"

Danish accents surrounded her, men panting, leather armor creaking, while far behind, and in another direction, swords rang against shields. Her father would scatter these invaders like unweaned pups!

Sheep made their low, startled noises as her captors made their way through the flock. The sharp, familiar odor of the livestock rose around them, and then receded as the heavily breathing men made rapid progress up-slope.

If any neighbor was going to spy her captors it would have to be now, before they reached the great, lichen-splashed boulders at the foot of the mountains, the paths she knew so well from the long summer twilights, climbing with Lidsmod up to their favorite, secret place, an elf cave just big enough for two people.

But there was nothing — no cry, and even the sound of battle was muted, was gone. She arched her body, freeing one leg.

She kicked.

Her captor struggled to seize her foot, grabbing and missing. She jacked her deerskin shoe hard into his manhood.

The stranger threw her down into the wet sheep-grass, with a deliberate, even movement. Two hard hands roughly cradled her head, and a voice hissed, "Do that again, beautiful prize, and I'll break every bone in your skin."

She grunted a retort through her gag. To her surprise her captor simply laughed and gave her a gentle pat through her hood.

Eight

Her bonds were loosened and retied, all the more tightly, using a length of some sort of fabric she did not recognize. Once again she was flung over her captor's muscular shoulder. Hallgerd tried to calculate where they were, how high above the village, the strangers' boots soft across the turf on one of the high sheep meadows.

A stream gushed, and splashed as they forded a current, Stag Brook, one of the many watercourses full of snowmelt this time of year. They were traveling faster higher, footsteps crunching snow. Hallgerd was surprised at the path they seemed to be following, a little used, rocky passage up through the mountains.

Hallgerd had heard of such captures, she reminded herself — they were the stuff of fireside tales, told to chill children and teach them caution. A jarl's daughter, forced into marriage or held for some political gain, would find herself powerless, far from friends and family. While the Norsemen of her experience treated neighboring women as respected equals, the women of far-off places were sometimes little more than prey.

Surely, she told herself, her father would retake her before the Danes could reach their ships.

By the time hands unfastened the sack from around her neck it was full morning, the sun nearly blinding off the mountainside snow. Someone behind her unknotted the leather gag and loosed the bonds around her wrists.

She blinked at the sudden sunlight, and kept silent. They were on the far side of the mountain ridge, out of sight of her village.

After her long journey, half-breathless and upside down, the sky swung slowly back and forth, and even the chirp of mountain birds sounded unfamiliar. Armed men were panting hard, flushed from their long climb. There were only half a dozen men, so badly winded that one or two slumped to the ground. Their armor was dark and well oiled, unlike the yellow, cracked armor of Spjothof's fighters. Their sword pommels were well-polished bronze. A man with long blond hair and gray eyes held forth a goatskin sack, and she accepted it, tasting water pleasantly flavored with mead.

This honey wine was not a common beverage in her own village, although foreign merchants sometimes traded it for cheese and sailcloth. The gods enjoyed mead every night, according to the poems. Only the wealthy men and women of the kingdoms to the south were so fortunate.

Which one of these men had carried her over the mountain?

"Did they hurt you?" the gray-eyed man inquired in that lilting, foreign accent of the Danes. His voice was soft, not unpleasing, and he wore a sword buckle of polished silver, an amber finger-ring on his hand.

Hallgerd said nothing. She could not trust herself to speak, and her bladder was about to burst.

Not far down the mountainside four ships nestled in the deep shadow of Wulffjord, the fjord to the south of her homeland. The tops of the spruce wood masts just caught the sunlight. Far in the distance was the early morning cooking smoke of the tiny village of Ard. She counted her enemy, and did not see enough to work so many ships.

"Tell me, jarl's daughter," he insisted gently, "if you have suffered so much as a single bruise."

She would choose her words carefully, and above all she would delay. Hallgerd expected to hear her father's battle cry very soon, and to see Hrolf's sword flash in the bright morning light. Now that she felt confirmed in her understanding that she was not going to be raped and butchered immediately, she tried to recall her father's ability to negotiate with difficult strangers. *Act as though the outcome is of no concern.*

And remember, her mother had always advised her, *who you are.*

Hallgerd's parents had often counseled her on her behavior in recent years, helping her to see that while she could continue to wear her hair loose around her shoulders like any unmarried woman, she would have to speak with a certain bearing. Hallgerd had a good example to follow: Rognvald's even temper, Sigrid's warmhearted gentleness.

And the legendary pride of her village. But it took an effort to keep her voice steady and speak as nobly as she wished. "No Dane alive," said Hallgerd, "has it in his power to hurt a man or woman from Spjothof." She said this to strike an attitude of calm indifference. She sounded, she thought, convincing. She began to feel the first glow of real courage.

The gray-eyed man smiled. "Then no one will do Rognvald's daughter any harm." He used the formal designation, *Rognvaldsdottir,* indicating that he realized her father was a man of name.

This polite way of referring to her parentage — fine courtesy by Spjothof standards — made her uneasy. Perhaps it was this easy reference to harm, or the extreme politeness, which Danes used to cover up their baser motives.

"If you have spilled one drop of my father's blood," she said, "I'll see your heads on stakes." She said this with too much passion for a noblewoman — there could be no mistaking her anger.

To her surprise, the gray-eyed man gave a bow.

Hallgerd's captors conferred with him, and with an apology one of them refastened her wrists. "Forgive me, pretty one," said the rough voice.

This was the one — the man who had threatened to cut off her nose and break her bones. This man spoke with an air of good cheer, as though she had agreed to take part in a rough game with well-established rules.

"Do you believe," asked Hallgerd, "that a few weak threads will bind the arms of my father's daughter?"

Her captor finished with his knots and stepped back. He was a well-built, suntanned man evidently proud of his smile — he showed nearly every tooth. "For a little while," he said, in a tone of gentle teasing. "If you will allow a seaman's hitch-knot to test your strength."

Like many seamen, his handsomeness was offset by a white scar, a straight line across his forehead. Many men carried such scars, the result of splintering oars or ship's strakes in collisions or battle. Oddly enough, this scar made him look less like a violent pillager and more like the good-natured shipwrights she had known all her life.

"These knots *do* hurt me," said Hallgerd, in the tone her mother used to get a shoemaker to set a lower price. It was not true — the cloth was some slithery, soft fabric, perhaps silk, although Hallgerd had rarely set hands on the precious cloth herself.

The gray-eyed man turned to his scarred shipmate with a troubled frown.

She spoke again, trying to sound as a noblewoman should, and doing, she thought, a good job. "They pain me very much."

The gray eyes blinked.

"They will cause me a bruise," she said. "And besides," she added, with what she hoped was a noblewoman's offhandedness, "I need to relieve myself."

The gray-eyed man nodded to Scar-Face. "Untie her," he said.

"I'll do that, Thrand, but she'll scamper," said Scar-Face. His voice was as rough as a file-stone, a man so strong, he could climb through an entire mountain pass without growing weary of his burden. But either the presence of his superior, or the proximity of the ships, softened his nature, and he did not frighten her so badly now.

She gave him what she hoped was a cool and level glance, and her scarred captor looked right back at her, smiling. She had an instant of impulse, imagining her hand drawing his knife from his belt, slicing his neck where the life throbbed.

"She's a noblewoman, Olaf," said Thrand. "Such folk expect to be well treated."

Scarred Olaf broke into a chuckle. He was a broad-shouldered, tall man, with the sort of muscles the best seamen develop from seasons of rowing. Hallgerd had heard ale drinkers describe a fighter named Olaf Bjornnson, often known as Olaf the Strong, who had sailed with Gudmund and killed scores of men. Such war tales were often unreliable exaggerations, she reminded herself, and a fighting man hired himself to various jarls, from season to season.

But perhaps this was the storied Olaf himself. It certainly was possible. This insight, she tried to reassure herself, did not trouble her at all.

"I think the ladies of Spjothof," Olaf was saying, "are at least half-wolf."

"Release her," said Thrand, with a soft laugh. "And I'll bet you a piece of silver she doesn't run."

"One whole piece of silver."

"Two," said Thrand, and the two men laughed together.

The sound of their amusement disturbed her, and she realized that calm as she tried to sound, she could do nothing to command these strangers, or to prevent them from hurting her.

Olaf unfastened her bonds and handed her the long length of silk, for certainly that's what it was, nearly two full ells in length. The shiny fabric was midnight blue, and at the same time it shimmered in the sunlight.

The armored men had fallen still, their faces expectant, while two muttered side bets to their companions.

Run.

Run, now — why are you waiting?

She should bolt across the mountainside, toward the distant, sulking hamlet of Ard, a smoky little settlement in the far distance. Which of these overmuscled, sword-clad men could catch up with her? Let them spear her in the back, or use a Danish weapon — an arrow or a sling stone.

She stepped behind a boulder furred with spring moss, the moss so fresh with life, it was golden. She knelt, disarranged her linen underclothes and, as she relieved her bladder, she had to admit how frightened she had been, and still was.

O Freya, goddess of the earth, she prayed. *Shall I run, and die in the attempt?*

Or stay, and pray that Odin shares his cunning with me?

Nine

Hallgerd's infant brother had died two summers ago.

It was cruel that the sunny season of tall, green-black birches and plush pastures saw Knut, the jarl's son, slowly develop a cough, then a fever, and gradually drift into a sleep from which he never awakened.

Hallgerd had helped her mother dress Knut's pale, shriveled body in the finest doeskin clothing. He was interred with a whale-ivory spoon and high-lace leggings in a burial mound that also protected the bones of his ancestors. Sometimes a seeker spent the night on top of such a burial mound, hoping that the dead would impart dreams that would allow a glimpse of the future.

Publicly, Hallgerd's parents had mourned the baby's death in the stoical manner expected of a jarl and his wife, but sometimes late at night Hallgerd had heard Sigrid weeping, and Rognvald joining her. Knut's cradle, made of oak, remained untouched in a corner of the longhouse. Hallgerd's family was proud, but it was a pride rooted in love for one another, and for their neighbors. The gods were enigmatic, but they respected human dignity, she believed, and they would not forget Hallgerd now.

It was this faith in her village, and in her father, that kept her from fleeing.

She returned to her captors. Olaf shrugged and laughed, accepting the loss of his wager with good cheer. Hallgerd would buy time, and give her father an opportunity to catch up with these Danes, following their trail.

"I know what you have tried to accomplish, Thrand," said Hallgerd, feeling once again a hopeful regard for this well-spoken leader. Surely the gray-eyed man with the gentle voice would be a reliable captor, someone with whom a jarl's daughter could negotiate. "And your good man Olaf — who, you should know, threatened to cut off my nose."

"No jarl's daughter could be deceived," said Thrand, accepting bright treasure, two fragments of silver, from Olaf's hand. Thrand wore a bright arm-ring, itself finely crafted silver, and his boots were horse leather, finer than any footwear her father owned. He added, "Especially one so beautiful."

A compliment was a gift, and Hallgerd gave a nod, secretly embarrassed by the bold eyes of these Danes.

Thrand said, "But now, let us hurry down to the ships."

"Where are you taking me?" she asked. If she delayed, enticing Thrand to engage in talk, she would buy time for her father and his men.

"To an endless banquet, Jarl's Daughter," said Thrand formally, "where you will be very happy."

"You set attackers on one edge of my father's village," said Hallgerd, "while you escaped with me on the other side, through the sheep to disguise your trail."

"Spoken like a seeress," said Thrand, without the least trace of condescension. "The rest of our battle force will come around the other side of the mountain. And we have to be joining them —" He made a gesture, polite but increasingly impatient, indicating the beautiful sailing vessels in the fjord below.

Thrand talked like a professional soldier, Hallgerd thought, a captain in a king's army, someone out of a foreign saga. Hallgerd had heard of such spear-bearing hosts, trained soldiers with matching helmets and well-practiced formations. By all accounts the men of Spjothof fought like warrior farmers, brave but with a manly casualness regarding strategy.

"You have gambled," she said, hoping she struck the right mix of confidence and pride, "that the folk of my village are fools."

"It was a reasonable hope," said Olaf, insinuating himself into the conversation. His rough laughter was joined by a few of the men.

"I will promise you a fat purse," said Hallgerd, keeping her voice steady, "if you return me to my father now."

"A purse fat with what?" said Olaf with rough good cheer.

A guard hissed.

Thrand held up one hand, his eyes searching the path they had just traveled. Every man listened, and Hallgerd joined them, holding her breath to make out a step high up the mountainside, and another, sharp pebbles scattering.

"Hallgerd, go with Olaf, if it please you," said Thrand briskly, "and find a comfortable seat in my ship."

A cry split the cool morning air, an unmistakable Spjothof accent, *"Thor by our side!"* — the ancient battle cry.

Hallgerd smiled grimly. Her father had recited this chant many times, around the kettle fire. It was the prayer the legendary Onund Stone-Ax had made when an army of trolls surrounded him. Onund called to the strong-armed immortal, and, with the thunder god's help, troll corpses choked the streams and turned the flowers along Spjotfjord scarlet. They were to this day the source of the finest red dye.

Hallgerd recognized Hego's voice. Surely many more voices would join in, every villager with a strong arm, overwhelming her captors.

The unmistakable sound of an ax against shield rang out through the morning air. The noise came from high up, and each Dane reached for a weapon.

Olaf seized her. "Come along, pretty treasure," he said with a laugh, a man not cruel, perhaps, so much as in love with his own brawn. He dragged her, picked her up, and swung her, kicking, but then, before he could take her far down the rocky slope toward the ships the sound of fighting made him turn.

He let her set her feet on the ground, keeping a seaman's grip on her arm.

"I'm here!" cried Hallgerd.

Above the sounds of a single battle-ax chopping a sword into bits, her voice echoed and reechoed off the mountains. Olaf pressed his weathered hand over her mouth, and her cries could only be prayers, now, muffled, soundless.

Father, I'm here.

en

Hego lay on the cool grass.

He did not know how he had gotten there, only that the soft tussocks of vegetation supported his head, and that he was grateful to the dark, wet field for embracing his body so gently.

His head hurt. He rolled onto his back and heard the sounds of a fire in the village, a great conflagration, like the giant bonfires of celebration that had followed *Landwaster*'s return a few short summers ago. Maybe the village was celebrating a wedding — *drinking a wedding,* it was called, the rowdy, all-night consumption of ale. Maybe that's what I was doing, Hego thought. I was dancing, whirling, and leaping, and I cavorted all the way out here.

Sheep surrounded him, the black-faced, well-nourished breed-ewes Hego knew were supposed to be in the pine wood pen in the village. The animals skittered one way and then another, bumping into one another, making that plaintive noise that Hego could not help imitating — feebly, not in mockery, but in wordless sympathy. He knew how they felt, the anxious, dumb creatures. Hego reached up to give a ewe a gentle pat, puzzled why the flock had been herded up onto the sheep meadow so early in the predawn.

His head throbbed, and when he put fingers to his scalp they came away sticky. He touched his forefinger to his thumb. He thrust out his tongue — it tasted very much like blood.

This was far from the first time that Hego had awakened under the dark sky in a field of gentle sheep-grass, but he began to knit together a memory of what had happened earlier that night. Soon he would sit up and really begin to make sense of what he was hearing, a sword ringing out against another sword, a spear striking a shield — it made a distinctive, hollow sound, even at a distance.

Perhaps the jarl had arranged a fighting contest — rough, merry games to entertain some important foreign merchant. The sounds of more combat drifted through the chilly darkness. The sheep parted, complaining, stirring anxiously, and a few men in stout, foreign armor hurried through the flock. One of the men carried a bundle over his shoulder, and the bundle was squirming and kicking. The bundle squealed — surely it was a woman. In the poor light

Hego could make out only a vague shape, but as the flock huddled together again in the wake of these strangers Hego felt the keen prick of curiosity.

And confusion.

In the neighboring fjord, behind the mountains that shielded Spjothof, was a tiny hamlet called Ard, from the old word for plow. This tiny collection of longhouses, nestled at the farthest end of Wulffjord, was known for its barley, which waved tall and golden on the hamlet's gentle slopes. The men of Ard held spitting contests each midsummer, it was said, unable to think of any intelligent sport. Spjotmen had always had summer spear-throwing games, and wrestling matches, and board games of strategy and capture. Spjotfolk prided themselves on their militant saga lore, and felt a sort of affectionate contempt for the village of Ard.

It was unheard of, Hego knew, for a group of these artless Ardmen to don expensive armor, and even less likely that they would try to creep into a village of legendary fighters and shipbuilders. Hego groped through the dark stems of grass, searching until he found Head-Biter, lying near a puddle.

Maybe tonight for the first time in their history the Ardmen had mustered a little spirit. Perhaps they had tired of their pudgy, argumentative brides and decided to steal one of Spjothof's beauties. It was a regretted but established way for an adventurous man to provide himself with a bride, and sometimes such a stolen woman lived long and happy years with her adopted household.

Hego hurried after this small band of raiders. He polished Head-Biter against the rough wool of his tunic and continued to think over the events of this night. He followed the band through the numbing cold of Stag Brook. How could they move so quickly? These strangers were athletes, long-legged and faster than any Ardfolk Hego had ever heard of. Hego had to run. Even so, they were well ahead of him, climbing up past the elf cave, higher, through the frost-crumbled, mossy rock of the mountain trail, speaking not a word that Hego could make out.

When one of them turned to survey the trail behind them, Hego melted into the shadows.

Not long afterward, as the first birds were stirring, one of the raiders turned again, and this time Hego was slow in hiding. On one side of the path was patchy snow, and on the other side a bank of ice, fanged with icicles. Hego knelt where he was, midpath.

The stranger stared, a long stone's throw ahead on the trail.

"What did you hear?" a voice asked, a foreign accent.

There was a muttered answer, and then the rear guard

turned and hurried after their fellows, leather armor creaking, feet splashing snowmelt all the way up the mountain ridge.

"Donsk!"

Hego said the word aloud, before he could shut his mouth, and one of the guards turned again, the first-dawn light reflected off the nasal-guard armor of his helmet.

Of course these weren't Ardmen — the thought had been ridiculous.

These men were Danes.

It all came back to Hego now, as he rose and sprinted to keep pace with the band.

He recalled how he woke, went out to drink well water, and met a sling stone with his head. No wonder he was bleeding! He should turn back to gather the village. There was no way one man could take on an entire band of sly, leather-armored Danes.

Not that Danes were feared, individually, the way one fears a berserker, or a veteran fighter like Trygg Two-Nose. Danes were famous for their rich foods, cow's milk cheeses, and pickled fish and bread. Danish bread was kneaded wheat dough, made with yeast and baked in loaves, not the hardy flatbread of northern villages. And they were famous for their treachery, fighting in trained armies with battle formations, always outflanking or using false retreats, hurling projectiles, and rarely giving way to tough-armed, sword-to-shield combat.

It was this very subtlety Hego knew he could not match. Matched with a normal warrior, Hego would teach him how to fight. He could outwrestle most men, but in the games of strategy, moving walrus-ivory pieces around to trap the opposing king, Hego had always accepted the affectionate consolation of his betters.

There was no time to go back for help. He hurried after his enemy.

Hego was breathing hard, and his head was bleeding again. The blood leaked into his swollen eye, but since this eye could not see well in any event, there was no great loss of vision. But Hego had sat long nights hearing stories about men foolish enough to take on too many opponents at once. Such fighters ended up in battle poems, but their flesh fed the crows.

He was on the slope high above the village now, the air cold in his lungs. This is how I will enter a battle verse, he thought. *Alone on the far side of the great Mount High-Seat he lifted his ax of noble name.*

Hego slipped on the icy trail, climbed to his feet, and made haste. He would call upon Thor at the last moment, the god of the strong arm and the boundary stone, the god who hates thieves and strengthens the man who defends his friends.

Hego stumbled, exhausted, crawling into the shadow of a boulder.

Their ships within view, the Danes were close enough to safety to catch a breath, sharing a drink from a goatskin sack. Hego crouched, breathing hard, leaning against a lichen-crusted boulder.

When Hego saw the Danes' captive, far below on the trail, he took a sharp breath and a firmer grip on Head-Splitter. Tears of outrage blinded him, and he had to wipe his good eye on his sleeve to clear his vision.

Hallgerd shook down her long, bright hair, and Hego cursed these Danes before Odin for setting their hands on the jarl's daughter. She was speaking to them, proud of bearing, Hego could see that, although he could not make out her words.

He could not linger here, crouching against the lichen-crusted rock. The wily Danes were glancing around, weary as they were, and soon someone would spy him, peeking out in his craftless, clumsy way.

Hego stepped out from behind the boulder.

He marched down the slope, his battle-ax in his grip, crying out before Thor for the mighty god's help. And a Dane, a red-bearded man, stirred, and climbed toward him, followed by a few others, all of them drawing swords, a few of them lifting skirmish shields.

The red-bearded attacker ran uphill, with easy, self-assured strides. He lifted his sword.

Hego sliced the shield through with one blow, and cut into the bone. Hego was singing. It was what he had been taught around the firelight, battle song giving courage to arm and ax. The red-bearded Dane struck out with his sword, a skilled counterattack, and Hego took a step back and planted his feet.

He killed the red-bearded man, clove his head from the crest of the helmet to the jaw.

And then, with Hallgerd crying out from below, the other armed men closed around him. Far outnumbered, fighting hard, Hego calculated how many he would take with him before he died.

Eleven

Hego was in the lead, and this surprised Hallgerd.

Indeed, not only was Hego leading the attack, no one else was following him.

The young man had polished an amulet for Hallgerd just a week past. Hego was always shy around the young woman, his voice soft, his eyes downcast. The jarl always sent his favorite blades to be quickened by the young man's whetstone. Every farmer was fond of Hego, but Hallgerd doubted that this youth was destined to earn his place in a heroic poem, and she was afraid for her good-hearted neighbor's life.

She could not bear to watch the fighting high above on the mountain trail.

And yet she did.

The mountain path wending upward behind Hego was empty, a long slope of shadows and lingering ridges of snow.

Hallgerd could not deceive herself. An impossible consideration could not be denied any longer.

Hego was entirely alone.

For the first time Hallgerd considered something unthinkable, something for which no amount of war lore or Spjothof legend prepared her: Perhaps her village had been devastated by these raiders. Maybe Hego alone had survived to press the pursuit.

Hego's song grew louder, the tune more erratic as he swung his battle-ax, chanting the poem of Thor before the mountain immortals, drinking from an ale horn the source of which was, unknown to the Thunder God, the entire blue sea. It was a poignant and powerful legend — the story of how even the great Thor could be deceived. Facing an unfathomable challenge, the mighty god had proceeded, swallow by swallow, to diminish the seas of earth by two fingers, and then half a hand, and more, failing the challenge but chilling the mountain gods with the sight of his determined strength. Spjotmen treasured this chant for moments of crisis, when the Norns of fate set an overwhelming enemy before them.

Before Hallgerd could offer a prayer for Hego's life, Olaf threw her over his shoulder and ran down the rocky slope, stones tumbling after them, a wet, noisy landslide of sharp rocks and ice melt.

Olaf's leather-booted feet thudded across a gangplank, and he flung her onto a large red embroidered cushion. Hallgerd could feel the shapes and textures of feathers within the soft pillow, and she stood up at once when she saw a *batr* — a small ship's boat — tied up beside the twenty-bench warship. Olaf gave a whistle, and a guard rose from within the boat. As Olaf instructed the young guard on some insufficiency in the knots that connected the small craft, Hallgerd looked around for a weapon heavy enough to crush the big man's skull.

This ship was richly carved along the sides, and decorated with bright hues, yellow, blue, and scarlet. The rowing benches were furnished with woolen blankets, and baskets of round cheeses were snugly stored in the stern. The ships that sailed out of Spjothof were never so well provisioned, and paint was hard to come by.

Hego's voice was silent now — she did not have to ask herself why.

Olaf was calling to her, telling her the eiderdown pillow was not as soft as she deserved but it was the best they could offer for now.

What Hallgerd wanted was a sword. Before she could find such a weapon the roar of several voices, both exultant and weary, reached the fjord from the mountain, reverberating throughout the fjord. From a cleft in the peaks known as Mjollnir-Rest, after Thor's great hammer, dozens of men in leather armor were streaming, running hard.

This pass in the mountains behind Spjothof was used only occasionally, by hunters of deer and wild goat. No invader had ever used it. Her neighbors had always told one another, half-believing it, that the god's great hammer rested there, protecting the village.

Each Dane wore a metal-studded helmet. Many boasted a bronze nasal-flange that extended down to offer protection to the face, and although many of the shields were badly hacked, only two or three men were wounded, the sort of superficial wounds that warriors made a point of ignoring.

This small army sprinted, stumbling and sweating, down the trail, and Hallgerd was sick with her continuing fear. No Spjotmen followed this armored, bristling band of fighters, and except for Hego and his ax, no force from Hallgerd's village showed itself.

If her father had breath in his body and blood in his veins, she knew he would be right behind this army of Danes, cutting them down as they ran. For the first time she let herself imagine in detail what must have happened as the large, diversionary attack drew the villagers into the dawn-gilded meadow.

Her father bleeding — too badly injured to lead a pursuit.

Or worse. She did not let this new, sickening fear take shape in her mind.

But it did anyway, against her will — the image of her father slain, his face pale and bloodless under the morning sky.

The small band of her captors joined this large body of men. Thrand in the lead, they stumbled, sweating, down to the ships. On the foot-trampled trail above, Hallgerd caught no sign of Hego's body. She prayed to the spirits that swept up fallen warriors and carried them to the Hall of the Slain. With tears in her eyes, she silently beseeched the immortals to seat Hego at the highest ale bench among the heroes of legend.

Oars were run out into the still, deep fjord, and the reflection of the surrounding mountains quaked and vanished as the white pine shafts sang through the oar holes and stirred the water.

Hallgerd's voice rang out.

It echoed from mountain to mountain, calling for her father, for her neighbors, and for the gods to come to the aid of her village.

Twelve

Gauk dreamed he was at home, hearth smoke stinging his eyes.

Opir, the village boaster, was saying that he could kill a she-bear twice as big as the one Gauk had slain, and Gauk's mother was challenging him jokingly, daring him to sail forth and give it a try. All the villagers were laughing, Snorri joining in, Gauk tasting the sweetest ale, and drinking.

Drinking deeply, filled with a thankful glow.

Gauk opened his eyes.

He was on the ice. He did not allow himself to dwell upon the starkly disheartening emotions this realization stirred in him.

He stood at once, stiff from the cold, the half-frozen bear hide beside him, and he told himself not to let his mind play upon the events of the day before. But even as he swore he would not recall any of it, it was all there in his mind. *Kill me and I'll change your life.*

The bear had seemed to speak from within Gauk's own soul. The young hunter could barely let himself recall the dazzling ease with which Whale-Biter had plunged all the way to the bear's heart. Or to consider yet again the numbing effort that followed, skinning the great carcass.

Snorri would have known how to stake the limbs and wield the cutting knife edge much better than Gauk, but his friend was reduced to a thing Gauk could not bring himself to look at, a poor rune of blood and rags. New fissures had opened as the sun set, the ice thawing with a sound like ugly music, and Snorri's body had slipped away, lost in a chasm.

Now the floe was ruddy with dawn, and the huge fissures wended in all directions. The fact of his solitude hit Gauk, and his great thirst. Women were allowed to weep, but men were expected to set their jaws and remain dry-eyed. Alone as he was, Gauk could not prevent sorrow from overcoming him again, and he wept. The memory of Snorri's laugh was agony.

A tern swept overhead, a white-feathered bird with a pronged tail and a black head. A flock of terns could indicate a school of fish, but a single bird, a recent arrival with the coming spring, could be an omen. Terns rarely touched earth or water, avoiding ice, plucking fish from the surface of the sea.

Gauk realized how hungry he was, and remembered climbing the cliffs of Spjotfjord with Snorri for the eggs of nesting birds. The yolks of the fresh fertile eggs had been so full of flavor!

Berserker.

Gauk could not quiet his sickening uneasiness. But at the same time, he wondered — wasn't there a certain thrill in thinking that the god would give him the power to kill men, whenever danger threatened? Wasn't there a basic fairness that Odin repay a bereavement with a great and terrifying gift? It was something the Spjothof elders had always said about the canny god — the divinity took something valuable before he would give any new gift. Gauk had paid in the rare silver of a good friend's life. Now he believed he would reap a just return as an Odin initiate, one of those who tie on a bear pelt and lose themselves in a fighting frenzy.

Usually when Gauk smelled sea or ice he could tell what animals had been feeding here, but today the wind was still. He thought of his father, dying far from his family, lost in the iron-dark sea. What prayer had Ara offered, so far from his friends and his family? The gods lived in a world of splendor, with the finest food and drink in beautiful ale halls, and it was difficult for a human to distract them from their pleasure with a few human syllables of devotion.

The small boat had been moored to a boat stake, and if the ice had not fragmented and drifted too badly, the vessel might not be far away. Errik, the village *skald* — poemcrafter — sometimes recited a verse about a charmed *skip* that could come when called. In a world of tools with names, and spears that a hunter could address like an old friend, such a story did not seem so impossible.

Gauk whispered the boat's name, *Stigandi — Strider*.

As a child his mother had given him walrus blubber to chew on, and even that simple food would have been welcome now. He gave Whale-Biter's iron spearpoint a wipe, breathing on it until the black gleamed. Some of the best metal fell, according to legend, right out of the sky. Surely Whale-Biter's point had come from among the stars!

Gauk rolled up the great pelt with difficulty, the fur thawing now in the sun. He began his trudge across the ice, dragging the fur behind him, mindful that with any step he could crash through the translucent crust and plunge into a void. His thoughts were all of beans served with mutton or boiled pork, and boiled cabbage. Even his mother's simple bread, ground peas patted flat and baked, would be delicious sustenance now.

The tern had returned, its shadow flowing over the glittering contours of the ice. The birds were not known as scavengers, but the searching glance of the winged creature took Gauk in, examining him as a source of food — or for some other reason. Odin was known to tease the folk he favored, placing rewards just out of reach, offering ironic discouragement, only to provide feast and firelight at the end of the long voyage.

The bird circled, out of place here, a single, wandering creature during the breeding season. Gauk was aware that such a creature might be yet another divine apparition, advising, teasing.

When he thought he saw the vessel at last, the blond wood dark against the floe, he fell to his knees. He blinked, rubbing his eyes, knowing that Odin deceived even as he rewarded, fed illusions, built up human hopes, only to dash them in rough chastisement.

He stood again, shivering, and shaded his vision with his mittened hand.

Thirteen

Gauk kept *Strider* on a steady course.

Navigation was easy as long as the low coast was within view, and the outlying islands. At times, as night fell, ice hove into view, recently calved blocks the size of warships. In the dark the crowds of icebergs took on a glowing solemnity.

It was dangerous sailing, and Snorri had always been better than Gauk at steering past trouble. Gauk tried not to think of how he would deliver the terrible tidings to Snorri's family. Gauk knew there was a bitter burden involved in telling bad news. There was a famous story of a grief-stricken family turning the messenger into an otter with a curse. The otter was later slain by a hunter, and the unwitting hunter was brought before the Althing — the summer meeting where disputes were settled — as a murderer.

When Gauk was thirsty he drank from one of the swollen goatskins of water Snorri had been careful to store in the sea chest days before. When he was hungry he chewed on some of the blood sausage Snorri's sister-in-law had made months ago, after pig-slaughtering day in the village.

The sausage was salty and chewy, but it was nourishing. Dark rose from the east, and a light rain fell. The weather cleared, and when Gauk looked back the polestar was steady, right where he knew it would be. The young man would have been grateful even for the companionship of Gorm, the most ill-humored of all the villagers. Even such a spiteful, unpleasant Spjotman would have been welcome on this silent voyage.

Morning and noon Gauk sailed.

When he slept, he reefed the sail and kept his hand on the steering oar, the way he had known Njord, the best village helmsman, to do during the long sealing expeditions Gauk had taken as a boy.

Gauk did not trust himself to sleep very deeply. He was afraid to dream of a home he might not survive to see again. But he was apprehensive about staying awake, too, unsure what new omen the god would display, what voice a puffin or a gull might put to use, just to startle a young hunter.

In a world of cordial ale halls and busy shipping yards, a few ports up and down the coast had an evil reputation. Here, along the northern coast of the land of Norway, was a tiny port where rowdy sailors sought easy pickings among fishing boats and hunting skiffs. The place was too ramshackle to have a name, although some Spjotmen laughingly called it *Losti* — Lust — because the pirates there were sexually rapacious as well as greedy.

As Gauk sailed the waters near Losti he heard a familiar cry. It was one of the raucous voices that had sung out similar crude threats when Snorri and he had sailed north.

"Where's your friend with the bronze laugh?" called one of the coastal pirates.

How many days has it been? Gauk wondered. It seemed so long ago. He felt like the hero who drank a lake of ale to win a bet, and woke to find all his friends withered and bent with age.

Two weather-stained ships loitered nearby, and one of them was setting a lumbering course that would intercept *Strider*.

Gauk counted the heads of his enemy — six men, not a serious fighting force, but enough to ferry stolen goods from ship to shore. And more than enough to manhandle one young hunter. Gauk was armed only with his hunting knife and Whale-Biter, and did not possess a shield.

"Where's your friend with the brave mouth?" this voice was calling. The crew put their heads together and burst out in laughter.

"Did he fall down on the ice?" sang out the voice. "Did

he hurt himself skinning a fish?" These questions struck his crewmates as the wildest wit, and men staggered, bent over with hilarity.

These coastal ruffians were notorious, but despite their ill fame they did succeed sometimes, according to rumor, in snaring a few disabled or novice boatmen. They operated general purpose ships, neither sleek enough to be warships nor stout-timbered enough to carry ore. Vagabonds were mistrusted, and outlaws were condemned to the most brutal fate, but the yearly law court had little power to enforce its will among men who dwelt on outlying islands.

Despite the evidently drunken condition of the man bellowing yet another question — *"Did you eat him for breakfast?"* — the man at the steering oar was holding an increasingly steady course, and three of the crew were making the unmistakable motions of men buckling on sword belts. Another made a thrusting gesture with a spear, warming up the muscles of his throwing arm. Gauk sailed away from the approaching ship.

Strider was fast, but as she sailed at an angle to the wind the boat began to take on water. The sharp spray slashed Gauk's face, and brine began to break over the sides of the craft. No one from Spjothof minded wet, and even the most seaworthy vessel took on water. Every villager knew how to bail, using the wooden water scoops with an expert hand.

But this extra load of water slowed *Strider,* and made her clumsy. The iron-voiced pirate was calling out that there was no fleeing, they had seen the bear fur rolled up in the prow. "Come about and let us feed you to the fish," he was saying with a laugh.

Gauk was determined to avoid trouble, and for a long time *Strider* stayed just ahead of the heavy ship. Many ruffians preferred sea fighting to land battle, so the ocean offered only a bleak refuge from experienced warriors, but the distant horizon was clear and cloudless. The pirate vessel had evidently been beached on many rocky shores — its prow was well scarred, and the ship cut through the swells with a stolid crash.

Snorri would have had little trouble eluding such a well-worn ship. Gauk, however, could not tease such speed from the vessel. More than once the ship's shadow fell over *Strider.* The armed men taunted Gauk with mock-encouragement. As *Strider* cut across the pirate vessel's path, working hard for the open ocean, the ship kept the pace, never slipping far behind. The armed men were growing uglier in mood as the chase wore on, the distant shore shrinking.

And the ship's helmsman knew how to travel the sea road, anticipating what moves *Strider* would make, cutting off the smaller vessel, and cutting her off again, until the sound of water rushing around the big vessel's prow was loud beside Gauk and spit flew down upon him from the cursing men leaning over the ship's side.

On Odin's shoulders sit two ravens, *Huginn* — Thought — and *Mummin* — Memory. From his high seat among the gods, the wisdom-loving Odin sees everything that happens. Gauk realized the fruitlessness of his flight, both from the pirates and from the god himself. Perhaps the outlaw ship was simply doing the violent god's bidding, testing Gauk's new gifts.

A spear, hurled from above, shivered in the small boat's planking. Another followed, just missing Gauk, and vanishing in the water. One of the pirates seized a long pole with a hook-and-bill of bronze, the sort of implement for securing floating objects from the waves.

The point of this gleaming tool was thrust at Gauk, and thrust again as the young man worked the small boat just out of range.

Gauk was growing angry now — at these guffawing, coarse seamen, at the gods, angry even at the vessel for not being more swift.

Gauk knew, from the poems he had heard since boyhood, that it would be in character for Odin to take on the appearance of an entire crew of furious, cruel men in order to make a game of trying out a new initiate's powers. Odin had long ago fashioned the world from the blood and bones of a giant named Ymir, and the god had surrendered an eye as the price for drinking from the fountain of wisdom. Odin was the most knowledgeable of all the deities, but he was also the one most in love with bloodshed.

This is where the god will give me strength, Gauk reminded himself. When I put on the bear belt and ask for Odin's strength, it will come.

Gauk shortened *Strider*'s sail. The vessel slowed, veering, and the ship bulked past, unable to slow down quickly enough. The pirates called out rude advice to their helmsman, and as the vessel came slowly about, Gauk stepped to the prow and picked up a black-stained packet of bear fur.

Gauk shook out a long, blood-grimed length of raw bear pelt. He had long dreamed of such a moment, but now that it was here he felt unsteady. He flung the length of ripe fur over his shoulder, fastening it with a bronze cloak clasp. Despite the chill in the air, the bear skin smelled of death.

fourteen

Once more, the shadow of the sea-battered ship fell over *Strider*.

The spearman in the prow called to the helmsman, words impossible to make out as the larger vessel's sail luffed and flapped in the wind. This was a rank, untidy ship, with a knotted length of *festr* — mooring rope — dangling from the side.

Gauk had heard the old poems, how a berserker actually feels the bear-spirit enter his body, changing his essence. To the bystanders — and to a startled enemy — an Odin initiate was a frightening sight. Gauk had heard this lore, but never quite believed it, even when Errik told one of his best poems, of ancient battle, an Odin initiate taking on an entire fifteen-bench warship, killing every warrior.

As the spearman made a halfhearted, lunging jab with the bronze-tipped weapon, a sound filled the sunny air like the panting growls of a she-bear when she defends her young. The fighting creature from *Strider* climbed over the side of the ship, and the spearman cried out for help.

The bear-man thrust once, and his spear sank deep into the spearman's breast. The berserker wrenched the spear free, and killed a swordsman with a thrust to the throat. A sword cut the air, missing badly, and the bear-creature's roar paralyzed this new attacker before he could ready another blow.

The creature who had been Gauk drew a hunting blade, slashed, and the swordsman fell to the deck, gagging on his own blood-rich howls. The helmsman leaped from the vessel, followed by his two remaining companions, but not before the bear-like beast slashed one of the fleeing men across the throat.

The two remaining dived into the sea.

No man could stay in the water long and live.

The cold already blanched the two still struggling on the surface, coughing, instantly too cold to beg for their lives. The bear-creature looked down at them from the ship, surprised at the shape of his own shadow on the water, a human being.

Fifteen

"Your father is unhurt."

Thrand offered Hallgerd this reassurance as the salt wind hummed. She wished she could trust his word, but said nothing. Silence, she believed, was her sole defense.

"The Spjotmen fought with spirit, but none of them was killed," he continued, gazing out over the rise and fall of the sea.

They spoke during the second sunset of their voyage, a flock of heavy-beaked puffins fanning out ahead of the ship.

"How can I believe you?" said Hallgerd.

The gray-eyed man considered, and asked, with a gentle laugh, "Are Danes famous as liars in your village?"

She did not respond. Danes were held in no high regard, but it would be bad manners to say so.

"I swear by Odin's high-throne," said Thrand, "that the only harm your village suffered, aside from a charred alehouse, was the loss of a wedding prize, Hallgerd — you."

She believed him. Every color in the air took on a richer hue, and the very flavor of the wind became more sweet.

This was the first confirmation Hallgerd heard that she was an intended bride. She knew there was a cruel honor in being such a valuable prize, and there was an implied promise that she would suffer no further physical harm. Of course, no woman from her village would ever accept such a marriage. She knew that her duty was to behave herself in a way that would reflect the dignity of Spjothof, and to buy time for the ships that would, eventually, avenge her capture.

"What war chief dares," she asked, "to think his bed can comfort me?"

She imagined Lidsmod arriving to do battle with a rich Dane, a fisherman with a fleet or a timber merchant grown wealthy. Certainly the man who sent an army to steal her away must be a landowner with chests full of silver heirlooms. Even the warriors he had employed had the robust, well-fed look of men who did not have to boil their own mutton.

But Thrand merely laughed, the soft, kindly chuckle her father used when he sought to end a conversation.

And he brought her a blanket of kid-wool and tucked it around her, his touch as gentle as his gaze.

Hallgerd looked skyward when all but the helm and the night-watch were asleep. Thor was the god most like a human being in his aspirations and pleasures. He loved to test his strength, rolling boulders and hurling his weapon, just like mortal men. He loved the smell of fertile fields after a long rain, and was saddened at a widow's tears.

Guide me to freedom, she prayed. *Give me the power to escape, and Lidsmod and I will name a son and a daughter after you.*

Hallgerd knew that if she fled now, trying to swim to the nearby rocky shore, she would lose her live in the profound cold of the water. And she would not be alive to witness the sea warriors of Spjothof when they wet their swords in the blood of these Danes. She longed for Lidsmod with his affectionate, thoughtful eyes, and his ready laugh. She wanted to breathe into his ear, even now, that she was well in body and spirit, and faithful to him.

Perhaps she would ask Lidsmod to spare Thrand. Certainly she would. In fact, these Danes were an oddly likable crew, despite their warlike nature. None of them was as quarrelsome as Spjothof's Gorm, or as tirelessly boastful as Opir, who did try Hallgerd's patience at times.

But the Danish laughter was softer than the hearty guffaws of her village, and their songs tuneful and touched with an almost unmanly sadness, the sort of songs Spjothof widows sang, or lonely wives. A tough lead oarsman from

Spjothof would never have sung the lilting poem that was the favorite of one scarred Danish seaman.

A sailor fell in love with an Arctic fox, in this chant, a creature who was a human female only during the months of summer. *"Come back to me, silver-whisper,"* sang the Danish warrior.

"Sing it again, Sverri," his shipmates would exclaim.

Morning, Thrand offered her a cup of mead.

The colorfully decorated ship that carried Hallgerd and her captors was called *Visunder* — Bison. Thrand was more than happy to point out the refinements of the craft, a thirty-four bencher, by far the longest Hallgerd had ever encountered.

Gilt paint scrollwork decorated a sea chest used by Thrand, and each of the other seamen had arm-rings or silver buckles kept carefully polished against the sea air. An eye on each side of the prow gave this ship some passing resemblance to a beast.

"She looks like a living creature," said rough Olaf, "doesn't she, Jarl's Daughter?"

Olaf was so openly proud of the vessel, and so boyishly in need of hearing it praised, that Hallgerd had to suppress a smile.

"In my village," she said, "any boy and girl can carve a bison out of whalebone."

But the half-resentful, half-pained look in Olaf's eye made her relent.

"She is a noble ship, it's true," she agreed, the way her mother would have, to spare even an enemy's feelings.

Indeed, the vessel's interior was drier and more comfortable than any seagoing craft Hallgerd had ever sailed before. Braziers of smoking coals warmed her hands and feet each morning, and Thrand offered her cups of fruit wine, a drink Hallgerd had heard of but never tasted in her life.

"Made of grapes," said Thrand, noting her expression of surprise.

She knew of berries, gathered wild during the summer. She had heard of vineyards in distant lands, but had never tasted their fermented juice. "I don't like the flavor."

Olaf gave his familiar grin, gazing down over Thrand's shoulder. "You'll get used to it," said the scarred seaman, "when you sit at your fine table."

Hallgerd gave what she trusted was a smile her father would approve.

Never, she thought.

Never, if it costs me my life.

Sixteen

When it was time for the evening meal, the sun-weathered sailing men opened wooden chests and brought out platters of loaf bread and slathered it with butter.

Butter was so rare in Hallgerd's experience that some farmers hoarded it like gold and paid off debts with small tubs of the stuff. Eating such treasure struck Hallgerd as an extravagant, reckless luxury, but the oarsmen around her bit into grand slices of bread and butter, laughing and enjoying one another's company. They placed bets on how long a seal would stay submerged alongside the ship, or which seabird would cross *Bison*'s wake first, just like the men of Spjothof, despite their Danish accents and unthinkingly rich diets.

Thrand gave her a linen cloth to dab the droplets of grape wine from her lips, and offered her cheese smeared with butter, smiling good-naturedly, and making no further threats. The soft-spoken man was the one who blew upon the hardwood coals until they glowed at dawn, and fastened a whale-skin over her shoulders in the gentle mist that fell one afternoon.

"You won't be cutting off my nose, Olaf?" asked Hallgerd as *Bison*'s sail was full bellied, the beautiful ship well ahead of the others.

"I would never have done such a thing," Olaf replied.

When she made no further remark, Olaf's smile become less certain. "It was a make-believe threat, Jarl's Daughter — nothing more than that."

Aside from Olaf, who turned out to be as much a hard-working manservant as captor, and Thrand, who finally poured a cup of Frankish wine so sweet, Hallgerd had to agree that it was delicious, most of the oarsmen ignored her. If the broad-shouldered helmsman met her gaze he would dip his head with a polite smile and then make every effort to find some point on the horizon to study.

One Danish warrior had been badly wounded in the fighting, a balding, heavily bearded man named Odd. A sword cut in his belly would not stop bleeding.

"I didn't feel the blow," he explained. "Or see it, until much later when my boots were full of blood."

Hallgerd knew it was a mortal wound but said nothing, feeling little but compassion for the Dane, and respect for the man's refusal to complain.

"I've been hurt much worse than this," said Odd. "My brother cut me with a scythe once, here — see the scar."

It was an old scar, a neat seam along his forearm. His friends agreed that they themselves had suffered many worse wounds, and Olaf said that he himself had been more badly injured a hundred times and that Odd had no need to worry.

But when Odd drank wine, it flowed right out the gash beneath his ribs. He laughed at this, and said he'd be able to outdrink even Olaf. But despite the encouragement of his shipmates, he fell into a slumber, his face swollen, his breath rattling.

It pained Hallgerd to hear Odd's friends tell their unconscious friend that they'd be home soon. "We'll turn the fattest pig on a spit," his friends told his senseless form. "We'll wear out the women and drink the wine dry."

When Odd breathed his last, Hallgerd expected to be the object of some bitterness.

There was none that she could detect. There was only a matter-of-fact sorrow as Odd's body was adorned with amulets and a good hunting knife, wrapped in seal skin, and committed to the black ocean swells.

Seventeen

For four days *Bison* and her companion ships followed the sea road south, swept along by a steady wind. Sometimes, along the coastline, a *kaupskip* — a merchant vessel — loomed out of a river's mouth, and received long study by the seamen. Sometimes a stained sail showed itself along the rock coastline, and they stared long after it.

On the sunny afternoon of the fourth day, the ship was readied for harbor.

Hallgerd did not need to be told what was happening. Cordage was uncoiled, chests freshened with oil, blankets shaken out and stowed, the entire vessel made as beautiful as the storied ships chosen for death voyages, the burials of grand ladies with objects of wealth and nourishment. The Danes were capable sailors, Hallgerd thought, but vain — not one of them could row for a morning without adjusting the creases in his tunic, worried that his clothes were getting stained by brine.

The Danish ships ran out their oars and entered a long, flat coastline. Hallgerd had heard the tales of attacks on such landscapes, and knew that Danes inhabited heath and bog land rich with birch forests. But the place *Bison* approached now was a habitation built up over the water on stout timbers, wharves and piers jutting out over the tide.

A white-timbered fortress angled up from the shoreline, and the silhouettes of spearmen caught the sun. Light glinted off iron spearheads as sentries gazed at the ship, and at her, strangers pausing in their conversation to point, and gawk. Was it only her imagination, or did the onlookers' lips form the words *the jarl's daughter*?

The days of good wind and kind weather had lulled her into childish confidence. Danish song and Danish gentleness had deceived her.

She was about to enter the town of an armed enemy.

Never had she been so afraid.

Eighteen

Bison made her way into the confined waters of the harbor.

Hallgerd had visited port cities before, with her father, although never one with such a tall timbered wall, each stave sharpened to a rugged point. This town gave every sign of being newly built, despite its impressive air of bustle and military might. Hallgerd knew that kings ordered the construction of such harbor fortifications to protect the mouths of rivers or defend their farmland.

"What place is this?" Hallgerd forced herself to ask, hoping her voice did not betray her anxiety.

"It is called Freylief," said Olaf. "It's an old town, but some of these walls have grown in the short time since I've slept beside my wife."

Hallgerd was familiar with the town's name, and felt a chill. The place was famous as Gudmund's stronghold. Olaf was plainly proud of his home port, and Hallgerd added, unable to keep the tension from her voice, "A mighty warrior must be jarl here."

Olaf smiled. "Gudmund wields a thirsty sword," he boasted.

Hallgerd was unable to keep herself from shivering.

Bison's oars stirred the quiet water. The sound of joiners' mallets rang across the harbor. Tiny boats serviced the larger craft moored along the wharf, heavy prowed freight ships manned by crews with black hair and dark eyes. No man was so busy he could not spare a glance at *Bison* and her companion vessels as they glided by.

Hallgerd could see no warships, a fact that gave her little happiness. The fighting ships were no doubt breasting waves, and bringing harm to distant places.

She counted the skips tied up along the wharf — small, sleek vessels Hallgerd could sail as well as anyone, if she had the opportunity. A single guard was posted near them, leaning on his spear.

When Hallgerd left the ship, more than one Danish seaman wished her well, a show of courtesy that touched her.

She felt little irony in replying that she hoped Njord, the god of ships and sailing folk, would strengthen every oar.

*   *   *

"You'll find us good folk," said Thrand, "if you are patient with us."

How strange the wharf felt under her feet! The hairy timbers were unmoving, and Hallgerd felt her legs search unsteadily, surprised at finding firm ground beneath them. *Land drunk,* some seamen called these first dizzying paces onto solid earth, but Hallgerd was careful to show no awkwardness.

As she steadied herself, a bearded, bear pelt–clad swordsman strode along the dock. This broad-chested townsman greeted Thrand and Olaf by name, and offered the seamen the goatskin he carried at his side. Hallgerd recognized a berserker's clothing, and observed him with interest and anxiety.

"Alrek," said Olaf, "I'm always glad to taste some of your mead."

Olaf wiped his lips with the back of his hand and offered the skin to Hallgerd, who declined courteously. "This mead is made from thyme honey," said Olaf. "Rare and sweet."

Hallgerd was ready to decline again, but she realized that noble manners required her to taste this offering. Not all honey is the same, she knew. The bees busy in the mountain bred a honey much more delicious than the domed hives set along a barley field. Alrek's mead was indeed flavorful — and strong. A few cups of this and even a berserker would be immobile.

To her surprise, Alrek the berserker bowed as she returned the goatskin to his broad, suntanned hand. It seemed that a

Danish Odin initiate was expected to be as well mannered as his neighbors.

"You've killed men by the hundreds," Olaf prompted cheerfully, "haven't you, Alrek?"

Alrek shrugged, either overly modest or recalculating his victories. Berserkers were famously spare with words. "By the many hundreds," said Alrek at last.

"I don't trust berserkers," Hallgerd confessed as Olaf and Thrand led her into the crooked lanes of the town.

Thrand said, "You are wise."

Spjotfolk expressed a degree of pity for town dwellers, tramping muddy streets, crowded around wellheads, and preferred the roomy, randomly situated longhouses of their own village. This Danish community had narrow, straw-strewn streets, massed with humanity and animals, and it smelled very much like a crowded habitation, ripe with manure and spoiled food. Goats bleated, pigs nosed a scattering of bright grain on the wet earth, and Hallgerd had an impression of buildings still freshly hewn, lumber bleeding sap and giving off the scent of just-cut forest.

Curious eyes followed Hallgerd, but she did not have far to go through the thronged lanes of leather-aproned craftsmen, all of them finding an excuse to step into their doorways as she passed. She carried herself with as much quiet dignity as she could. The smell of malt was in the air, and the *tink-tink-tink* of a tinsmith's hammer. The townsfolk wore *vadmal* — brown homespun wool — just like the men and women of Spjothof, although Hallgerd reckoned that the quality was trade-worthy and far from cheap. She tried to read her fate in the alert faces she passed, but she could see only recognition.

And something else. Respect, perhaps. Or even envy. The townsfolk knew who she was, and why she was here.

She herself knew nothing.

Accompanied by Thrand and a few seamen from the ship, she found herself treated as an honored guest, the phalanx of armed men like body servants, pointing out the puddles of pig manure in the street so she could avoid them. A woman dressed in the drab, shapeless tunic of a slave ground grain in a stone quern, and other slaves swept thresholds and emptied slops into the street.

The two white-aproned women fell quiet as Hallgerd passed. The gray-haired woman leaned toward her companion, and Hallgerd read the words on her lips: *The stolen bride.*

The jarl's daughter hoped that, in her borrowed *grafeldr* — gray travel cloak — her hair gathered modestly under her hood, she represented her village well.

Which crooked street, Hallgerd wondered, was the way to freedom?

And how far could she run?

Thrand and the armed men led Hallgerd to the *stokkr* — threshold — of a pine-timbered longhouse.

The threshold was the traditional boundary between the domain of women and men. Hallgerd reckoned that if this town was very much like Spjothof, the house guard who opened the bronze-hinged door was subservient to the keeper of the house, just as Hrolf accepted his instructions from Hallgerd's mother and cooperated agreeably with Grettir.

Hallgerd took a moment before she drew any closer to the building, pointedly ignoring Olaf's whispered, *"Hurry!"*

Bright red paint decorated the doorposts, a serpent design. Black wings were stirring in the golden thatch of the long-house, two ravens perching on the eave, lifting their metallic voices to each other, and to the knot of humans below.

It was common for birds to take up residence in a town. Some villages were famous for the white, long-beaked cranes that inhabited the roofline, and some houses were visited by owls. Certainly the raven was a fairly ordinary creature. But the bird could also be a messenger from the One-Eyed, and Hallgerd offered the unspoken question to this handsome, blue-black pair: *What will happen to me?*

A woman opened the great wooden door.

The housekeeper of a great house was either a high servant or an important relative of the nobleman who owned the dwelling. The woman's eyes flickered up and down Hallgerd's cloaked figure, a measuring look.

The housekeeper did not leave the shelter of the door frame, the frontier of her authority. Neither did she make a move to admit Hallgerd. Thrand gently tugged the hood from Hallgerd's head, and the housekeeper gave Hallgerd a brief smile, reserving a sharp glance for the armed men who accompanied her.

"Who have you brought to my mistress's house?" said the housekeeper.

"It's the beauty from Spjothof, Syrpa," said Thrand. "As anyone with eyes can see."

"Where have they found you, child?" asked Syrpa, not unkindly, putting her hands on her hips.

"We brought her kicking and squealing," Olaf said.

Syrpa lifted an eyebrow, and Olaf fell silent.

Syrpa's tone was measured, but far from unfriendly. "I've never met an honest seaman," she explained to Hallgerd. "They would lie to the moon if they thought it would win them silver. Who are you?"

Hallgerd spoke. "My father's daughter wishes you a good day."

At these words, perhaps convinced by Hallgerd's accent, or by her bearing, the housekeeper stepped to one side, making an unmistakable gesture of welcome.

I won't go in.

Not with breath in my body.

For several heartbeats Hallgerd would not cross the threshold. Whispers in the smoky interior told her that serving men and women were watching and that whatever she did next — whether an act of cowardice or courage — would be long remembered.

"Only three more strides complete your journey," prompted Thrand. "I promise you — no one will hurt you." No doubt the kind, gray-eyed man had been promised a purse of some rich coin on delivery, but Hallgerd considered what a good-humored, considerate sea host Thrand had been.

Not every captor was cruel, and stories abounded of honorable warriors who won fame by stealing future brides. Some songs told of such fighting men falling in love with their captives, and of their hostage's warm feelings in return. While Hallgerd felt no such tender feeling for Thrand, she was sorry to bid him farewell.

"I thank you, Thrand," said Hallgerd, continuing to employ the highest speech she knew. "And I will implore my father, when he burns this city to the ground, to spare your head."

Thrand's gray eyes were intense with some unspoken message. His lips parted, but he said nothing further.

Hallgerd stepped *fyrir innan stokk* — over the threshold — as the huge door shut.

Nineteen

Hallgerd counted six windows in the smoky hall, all of them stoutly shuttered.

Figures paused in the thick hearth smoke, and leather soles padded this way and that in rooms beyond. The number and variety of furs on the floor and spread across the walls, and the presence of separate living chambers across the smoky interior, told Hallgerd that this was a richer and grander house than any in Spjothof.

"Please forgive me for questioning you so," said Syrpa. "Seamen have been known to pass off any fine-looking woman as a noble daughter, simply to collect their fee."

The benches set out beside tables, and the storage chests along the walls were familiar-looking, but as Syrpa led Hallgerd into a side room, the young noblewoman was aware that despite her status as a captive she was also a war prize, a jarl's daughter, and enjoyed a lofty status.

*   *   *

Hallgerd dined at a broad table, supping on a large piece of fish that had been softened with warm butter. It was delicious. So was the honey wine Hallgerd accepted with thanks, and the ample slice of brown wheat bread and butter.

Servants stole glimpses of her, but the presence of Syrpa at the side, cutting another serving of loaf bread, gave Hallgerd the continuing impression that she was both guest and captive. Chain mail gleamed in the doorway where armed guards stood duty.

"Are you unhurt?" the housekeeper was asking. She gave her words particular weight, and Hallgerd knew that she was asking if her captors had taken sexual advantage of her.

Hallgerd did not answer at once. She knew that silence continued to be a defense, perhaps the only recourse left to her. And possibly Olaf deserved some punishment for his braying laugh, even though she already missed soft-voiced Thrand. At the same time, Hallgerd was aware that Syrpa could be a source of information — and perhaps even prove to be an ally.

"I am not pleased," said Hallgerd.

"Have they caused you any injury?" said the serving woman. "If they have, my mistress will turn each one of them on a spit over a fire."

Just as the men and women of villages like Spjothof were reputed to be drunkards, the Danes were imagined to have large appetites for women. Hallgerd was not, however, a maiden, having spent time with Lidsmod under the sky and in their favorite cave. If this would render her an unfit bride, Hallgerd would happily tell this servant about her deep love for the man she hoped to marry.

"They have hurt me, Syrpa, by stealing me from my father's house."

"Of course," said Syrpa, and in this eager but flat-toned agreement, Hallgerd could take little comfort.

"What will happen to me?" asked Hallgerd.

"The lady of this house will see you when she wishes," said Syrpa, with the well-trained air of a veteran retainer, neither friendly nor forbidding.

Hallgerd could scarcely bring herself to frame the question, but needed to seek information regarding the famous war chief. "Is Gudmund the Fair still a killer of men?" she asked.

"Gudmund sails with the best warriors under the sky," said Syrpa properly, but with an air of cordial calm.

"Has this great jarl," asked Hallgerd, "sent for me?"

Syrpa's features dimpled with something like a smile. "Gudmund? Oh no, dear child, not that noble warrior." She laughed, real amusement lighting her eyes.

"Then who has dared to raise his hand against my village?" asked Hallgerd, her pride stung.

"Your hostess," said Syrpa.

Hallgerd had always enjoyed the long winter nights playing word games with her friends. Now she took no pleasure in such drawn-out conversation. "My hostess, and your mistress," said Hallgerd.

Syrpa gave a bow of assent.

Danish towns were what Spjotfolk called *deep-wealthy*, well appointed with both furnishings, weapons — and thralls. But she understood, too, that it was very unlikely that a jarl's daughter would be stolen simply to adorn this timbered hall as an exotic bond servant.

"I was raised by my family housekeeper," said Hallgerd, hoping to form some understanding with this imposing chief servant. "A gentle woman, named Grettir. Kind, and wise. I shall miss her very much, until I see her again."

"You can send for her," said Syrpa. "After you have learned to call this place your home."

Hallgerd chose her words with a certain delicacy. "Syrpa, does your mistress command ships?"

"Her father sails ships from Frisia to the Seine," said Syrpa. Then, perhaps aware that she had confided too frankly, she added briskly, "You will bathe when you have eaten. And afterward I shall show you your bedchamber."

"I shall bathe when I choose," said Hallgerd. She took a sip of mead, a drink she rarely tasted, marveling at the flavor. "Who is it, Syrpa? Who has committed this crime against my village?"

"Arnbjorg, Gudmund's daughter," said Syrpa confidingly, lowering her voice. "She seeks a wife for her son."

One of the serving thralls had a patch of dark red on the back of his tunic, a long curve of dried blood. Some mistresses punished slaves with whips, Hallgerd had heard, but most did not. Any show of uncontrollable emotion toward servant and neighbor alike was considered bad manners among the Norse. Still, it was not hard to imagine what cruelty might take place in a house owned by the legendary fighter.

Hallgerd managed to keep her composure. "I do believe I misunderstand you."

"You will marry into Gudmund's family!" whispered Syrpa.

Hallgerd's throat closed, and she felt the candles around her dim.

"I will pay a heavy price," said Syrpa, continuing to whisper, "if my mistress ever guesses that I've told." She paused, perhaps taking in the sounds of the timbered dwelling all around. Then she said, "Gudmund and his family want to ensure a strong alliance with Spjothof, so that your brave village will never again harm Danish settlements."

"Why is there such a need for an alliance?" Hallgerd managed to ask.

"The Franks are newly powerful, armored and carrying heavy swords. They are seeking new territory themselves, from the south, and need careful watching."

Hallgerd appreciated the flinty logic of such reasoning. She had heard Rognvald discourse on the Franks over ale, and knew that many forced marriages resulted in strong bonds between old adversaries.

The young noblewoman put her hand over the housekeeper's work-reddened fingers. Such servants gave orders to a staff of servants and thralls, and were respected by fighting men and noblewomen, but there were limits to their power. Hallgerd suspected that Syrpa had come close to violating some confidence by saying too much.

Hallgerd asked, "What is he like, this man I am expected to marry?"

But Syrpa said no more.

Twenty

Hallgerd's bedchamber was adorned with plump pillows and a bear pelt on the floor, an extravagant fur she was reluctant to tread on. Cunningly woven cloth decorated the walls. The red-and-blue-dyed *litklaethi* — colored fabrics — were brilliant evidence of the household's wealth.

Soapstone craftwork was displayed on a side table, including a well-wrought carving of Sleipner, Odin's eight-legged horse. A *taflbord*, for playing games of chance and strategy, was set out, as though to reassure Hallgerd that she would never suffer the stark boredom of a prisoner. The game pieces were agate and jasper, rare minerals in Hallgerd's world.

Serving women brought her a pitcher of wine-and-water and a heated rock, wrapped in homespun, to warm her bedding against the evening chill. These servants lowered their eyes in her presence and spoke in the soft, deferential tones not even the lowliest bond servant used in northern villages.

"Is there anything further we can bring you?" asked one of the young women.

"How many spearmen guard this hall?" asked Hallgerd.

"Enough, if it please you," came the predictable response.

Hallgerd thanked the servants and they left her, closing the door carefully. The iron chime of a key ring and the metallic click of a lock told Hallgerd that she lacked the one luxury she would have chosen — her freedom.

She pressed her ear against the locked door and heard only muted voices, and the sounds of benches being pushed against the walls as the day drew to a close. There was another sound, too, the harsh voice of Olaf murmuring confidingly to someone in the distance. She could almost make out the words.

Her bedchamber had no window, but she could tell, by the drowsy murmur of the folk in the hall beyond, that night was deepening, and soon everyone but the sentries would be asleep. The butt of a spear tapped the floor just outside her door, and leather armor creaked.

An inner argument had begun playing through Hallgerd's mind.

If she could dally with the people of this house, and put off the hour when she met her intended husband, perhaps she could pass the coming days pleasantly enough. After all, if no one in Spjothof had been seriously hurt, there was only her own capture to be avenged. Perhaps even Hego had only been injured, his life spared. She allowed herself to consider Thrand's gentle manner. Surely such a leader would not have permitted wanton slaughter. She was being treated with queenly comforts, and aside from her loss of freedom, she had an opportunity to enjoy soft-spun blankets and sweet wine.

She could rest for a few days, before planning her escape.

In her sleep, the bedchamber seemed to be in constant motion, rising and falling, floating on the choppy surface of the sea. Olaf was laughing, and Thrand speaking softly, a message she could not hear. Hallgerd dreamed of wings, blue-black, and a black beak.

A large bird, a raven.

The raven spoke to Hallgerd, and she could nearly make out what the bird said, her pulse pounding as she strained into the sound of wind, trying to catch the raven's warning.

Lies, Hallgerd.
He lied to you.

She woke suddenly.

The key ring rattled, and Syrpa hurried into the chamber.

"Be quick!" said Syrpa, her own hair undone and flowing down her shoulders. "We mustn't keep Arnbjorg waiting."

The continuing darkness of the hall beyond, and the first tentative stirrings of birdsong, indicated the earliness of the hour.

Hallgerd was on her feet, body servants helping her into a new chemise of pleated linen. She felt herself being hastily assembled, suddenly wide awake, like a child's puppet sewn together in an instant. Her feet were thrust into lamb's wool hosiery, and a long blue dress was pulled over her, tugged and fastened.

The dress had trailing sleeves — a fashion, Hallgerd had been told, among wealthy ladies. The garment was suspiciously well-fitting, even when the laces down the back were pulled tight, and Hallgerd wondered how many merchant ships had carried spies from Gudmund's family, silently measuring Hallgerd with their eyes.

Her hair was quickly brushed, and Syrpa eyed her critically, making minute adjustments in the dress.

I will see Gudmund's daughter when I choose.

This was what Hallgerd wanted to say.

But the armored house guards kept a firm grip on either arm as they led her into the hall, toward a blazing fire in the center of the room. There, a woman in an ashwood pale dress was gazing into the flames, iron rod in hand, heating the end to scarlet in the coals.

"Is this she?" asked the woman.

Syrpa made a murmur of assent.

"Step closer," said the woman by the fire, "so I can see you."

Twenty-one

A sound startled Gauk, something breaking the surface of the ocean.

He worked the sail so the boat slowed. The day was bright, but he had heard of sea thieves who used one-man vessels to steal up on unsuspecting sailors. Gauk had drowsed, just for a moment, and now his heart raced.

With a snort, and a flurry of white water, something was nearby, salt spray bright in the air.

A seal's head broke the surface of the sea.

He was a creature so dark, the whiskers on his snout were silver, his teeth white and perfect, the ridged interior of his mouth bright pink.

"Are you lost?" Gauk asked, his query a dry rasp.

It was a question of some weight. Gauk himself would have been lost, if it were not for the traditional way-poems that every child in Spjothof knew by heart. These songs were a method of remembering navigational clues — landmarks and sea features. They contained information about rocky outcroppings and towns all the way from the farthest north, south along the Danish kingdom, to the land of the Franks.

> *Keep the seabirds,*
> *the guillemots and their kin*
> *within your mast's shadow*
> *sailing north, sailing south.*

The seal parted its bristly snout. Was this animal, too, another Odin presence?

Gauk tossed the butt end of the remaining blood sausage into the water. Some hunters would have thrust a harpoon into the beast as it nosed the morsel — seal skin was valuable, making excellent covering against wet weather. But Gauk made no move to reach for Whale-Biter. Some sailing folk believed that seals were men or women who took to the sea in the form of these long, sleek creatures for the joy of it.

Gauk did not quite believe this, but he welcomed the companionship. The seal plunged deep, pirouetting beneath the boat, trailing a long string of bright bubbles, and vanishing beneath the swells.

Gauk envied the seal its athletic innocence. Gauk had felt innocent, too — before Odin had made him a killer of men.

He did not allow the images from the previous day to enter his mind, an act of denial that took great effort. The men in the water had tried to swim, but the cold stiffened their limbs, until the dark sea swallowed them. Gauk felt soiled, and badly shaken.

But at the same time he felt a deep wonder, too, and an ugly joy. Now that Gauk was bear-clad, no man would ever insult Gauk or his village to his face. Even seasoned fighters would step aside when Gauk entered an ale hall, an ursine pelt over his shoulder or around his waist. Gauk would not feel the boyish awe most youths feel toward veteran fighters and their war tales.

Strider sailed itself, with very little prompting from him. Blood spatters dried on his shaggy coat, and on his mittened hands. The blood flaked off and turned to red dust, but it left stains. He wore a sword at his hip now, taken from a pirate's dead body.

Life as an Odin initiate held a certain grim thrill. But the reality of such a life tasted bitter now. Stories were told of berserkers who were overcome by bear-spirit during feasts and weddings, butchering innocent celebrants. Such men quickly became friendless. There were stories of brave voyagers who killed berserkers on sight. Gauk himself had seen a berserker on the wharf of a southern port, half-killing a man with his naked fists while his neighbors tried to haul him away. Gauk was afraid of what he had become.

The thought was foreign to the strong young hunter, but he could not put it out of his mind: Perhaps he should fall upon his spear, here, on the open sea. It would be better than returning to his beloved village and becoming a danger to his comrades. Gauk had once entertained a secret whim of being such a killer, and now he would pay any price to return to his former life.

The seal appeared again, and Gauk wondered if this animal was now going to utter some portentous speech. The creature looked happy, alive to some delicious secret.

"Tell me what will happen," whispered Gauk.

Twenty-two

◆ ◆ ◆

It was a sun-drenched afternoon.

The little town of Blot nestled at the edge of a harbor. The low hills around the settlement were rocky and lush green, with a line of dark forest and fuming hot springs high beyond.

The seal had offered no syllable of prophecy, but Gauk knew where to get help. Spjotfolk had a reverence for this northern village. The town's name meant worship, sacrifice, and the place had for generations been associated with Odin. Legend had it that one night-dark winter day a fisherman, mending an *eikja,* a crude sort of boat, spied Odin walking along the frozen land, carrying a two-pronged stick to keep from slipping on the ice.

Blot had been the home of the famous seeress Steingirdr Hakarsdottir, who had foretold the kingship of the old king of Denmark Angantyr. Possessed by envy and frustrated spite, one of Angantyr's rivals had killed the seeress, cut off her head, and thrown it onto the sea. Within weeks the foolish rival had gone mad, hearing the seeress's voice in every hissing wave.

A new seer named Jarn Ketilsson lived in the hills above Blot, and for a price this man was as prescient as any prophet who had ever drawn a breath. The story was that this seer had burned out one of his own eyes so he could resemble Odin. Other stories told that he had cut off one of his ears, or axed off one of his hands. In any event, Jarn was reputed to be a knowing and austere man, who turned many seekers away from his door. His powers were expensive, but insight into the future was considered by most Norse a gift beyond reckoning.

Gauk tied the boat against the rude wharf and hefted his heavy load, the uncured bear pelt, staggering under the burden.

A man planing a ship's spar with a two-handled blade looked up at his step.

"Good shipwright," asked Gauk politely, "please tell me, which is the way to the house of the seer Jarn Ketilsson?"

The shipwright eyed Gauk with an air of cheerful suspicion. "The seer consults with princes," he said, running a thumb along his blade. "The sons of jarls might be allowed into his company. A sea leader with an armed fleet waiting might, possibly, be allowed to put his head into the doorway of the seer. But not, I think, an ordinary hunter."

Troubled by this, Gauk set down the heavy pelt and straightened, easing his back.

"And Jarn," the shipwright continued, "is not pleased at the sight of a bear fur, hunter. Anything that reminds Jarn of a bear killed, or hurt, or even troubled, offends him greatly."

Gauk sighed, feeling dismal, unequal to the challenge of an audience with the famous seer, but willing to pay any price. "What can I do?"

Perhaps something about Gauk's downcast eyes touched the shipwright. The man turned away and examined the spruce wood spar. "You'll find Fat Grim at the top of the road. He's an honest trader and has been known to set his hand on silver."

The merchant who fingered the bear pelt did not wrinkle his nose at the overripe stink.

He probed and pinched the fur, but made no remark at the rancid, black flesh along the edges. The luxurious hides of black fox and beaver hung head-down from the walls of Fat Grim's dwelling, and squirrel pelts were spread on wooden stretchers. In Spjothof such a store of furs would have indicated a dazzling degree of wealth. Fat Grim was a deep-chested, hale man with a gray-streaked beard. He was, as his name had promised, a portly individual. He ran a hand over the thick, bright fur, and noted the place where Gauk had cut it.

"It would have fetched a better price if you'd not cut it so," said the merchant as Gauk took a seat on a three-legged stool.

"No doubt," said Gauk. "I would like to sell the pelt — but keep the paws at my hip."

He had always left bargaining for sailcloth or salt cod to Snorri, who had always had the cheerful retort and the off-hand, easy manner that brought a price lower and lower, with laughter and gentle teasing on both sides.

Fat Grim was an old hunter himself, judging from the scar that ran along one arm, a long, pink cord from wrist to elbow, the sort of wound a boar made, slashing with his tusks. The grizzled merchant touched the walrus scar in the bear pelt and said, "You did not kill this bear all alone."

"I hunted with a friend," said Gauk. "But as the Norns wove my fate, I had no choice but to kill him with my own hands."

Gauk had heard hunters and warriors describe their feats with a terse humility, and always had admired the matter-of-fact stoicism of such men. Gauk had never anticipated sounding like this himself.

"No doubt that is why you wanted to keep the paws," said Fat Grim, indicating the remnant at Gauk's feet. "As a memorial to your friend."

When Gauk smiled, but did not make any further remark, the merchant reached for a pitcher and poured ale into a wooden cup. He offered the drink to Gauk, who accepted it in both hands, as good manners dictated. He waited until the merchant had poured a cupful for his own enjoyment. Drinking was rarely casual among Norsemen.

The two drained their cups. It was good, sweet ale. Fat Grim poured them new servings and they both drained their cups again — to show restraint in drinking was unmanly and discourteous. Grim wiped his heavy mustache with his sleeve, took in Gauk's sword and the dried blood on his tunic, and gave a belch, the sign of a good-hearted appreciation for drink.

"Six seal pelts will fetch an *eyrir* of silver among the Swedes," said Grim, "but try to sell seal pelts to the Franks and they'll ask you to throw in a keg of boat pitch, something they could use."

Gauk said nothing, aware that he knew too little of such things.

"Bear pelts, though, are a different matter."

"How much can you give me?" Gauk asked.

Grim raised a finger, silently counseling patience. "Perhaps you would sell the sword strapped around your middle."

"I won this —" *with bloodshed,* he nearly said.

The trader sighed. "The Franks have rare ladies. Cream-fed noble folk. They take a special joy in feeling bear pelts against their skin."

"So how much —"

"I've heard such Frankish ladies dream of cloud-borne pleasures when they drowse on such furs."

"I've never met a Dane, let alone a Frankish lady."

Grim's eyes grew small as he offered a compassionate smile. He added, "But there are no Franks in Blot, my brave hunter, and not likely to be until much later in the summer — if even then, when their ships call this far north."

"The seer," said Gauk, "will want a plump purse before he'll agree to the son of my father." *Son of my father* was the polite, formal way of referring to oneself. Gauk felt disconsolate, and more in need of a seer's advice than ever.

Grim poured them both more ale. "It is at this point in the bargaining," said the trader, "that a merchant from one of those fjords to the south cheats the youthful traveler." They both drank. "They give the hunter a bag of resin and a tethered goose, and weep that the price is too dear."

Gauk burped. The drink was strong. "It is a pity to cheat a traveler."

"And the gods," said Grim, with a bright look in his eye, "loathe a crooked merchant."

"I've heard that is true," agreed Gauk.

"Although none are cheaters," said Grim, "like the pelt buyers of that coarse, smoky hole called Spjothof."

Gauk stood, his fists knotted.

 Twenty-three

"What did my ears just hear?" Gauk asked, the old formula for asking for an insult to be repeated.

"I said no one cheats," said Fat Grim, "and no one fights as badly as the weak-kneed men and women from the stink hole called Spjothof."

Gauk kicked his stool to one side.

To his surprise, Fat Grim was laughing, slapping the table with his hand.

"Sit down, my good friend — and accept my apologies," said the stout merchant.

Gauk made no move.

"I recognized a Spjotman when you stepped through my door," said Fat Grim, "and I played a game at your expense."

Conversational sport was prized among all the Norse. Men and women would sit around the simmering stew pot and enumerate the virtues of a certain leader, or ship, or village, and sometimes such talk turned just the opposite in tone, and involved colorful but well-intended mockery.

"Who else but a Spjotman," Grim continued, "would wear such a fine herringbone-weave tunic?"

"The men of Blot take humor in rough ways," said Gauk, after a silence.

"We do indeed," said Fat Grim. "I apologize again to my brave guest."

Gauk sat. He felt more than a little embarrassed to have been so easily offended at such a traditional form of teasing. Calm in the face of word-sport, like a strong head for drink, was widely admired.

"And to repay you for your patience," said Fat Grim, "I shall offer my advice."

Gauk eased himself into a bubbling spring, letting the warm water knead him, the heat of the merry waters seeping into his muscles. Baths were enjoyed throughout the Northland, and the time after the evening meal was often referred to as *badferd,* bathtime, so frequently did men and women enjoy such quiet pleasure. Fat Grim had cut a slice of boiled seal steak and let Gauk wash the sweet, close-grained meat down with yet more excellent ale. Gauk felt that he had stumbled upon the best hospitality a traveler could desire.

Beyond the bathhouse, through the cracks in the birch wood shelter around Fat Grim's spring, Gauk observed the merchant's female house servants at work on his own blood-stained clothing, beating the garments with the *vifl*, the traditional laundry bat. When the clothes were clean, the house servants hung them on a line between two poles. Gauk watched his tunic and leggings and coarse-woven linen underclothes dance madly, alternately full of wind and empty, an amusing sight, like the crazy, spirited dance Gauk's neighbor Hego did when he had a belly full of drink.

The span of rank bear skin waited in a corner of the bathhouse, rolled tight.

Because people bathed frequently, and streams of warm water flowed from the numerous springs up and down the mountainous coast, cleanliness was both widely admired and expected. Fat Grim's advice that a clean, well-laundered supplicant would be more acceptable to the seer had been wise, and Gauk was grateful. He soaked for a long time in the purling waters.

A *badkona,* a bathing servant, brought Gauk's newly cleansed garments to him, and the pretty, dimpled young woman helped Gauk into his clothing. Unused to the attention of servants, Gauk thanked her. That the servant was a comely woman made his self-conscious thanks all the more heartfelt.

"It's all a part of my duty," she answered, using a word Gauk knew well, *morginverkin,* daily duties varying from splitting wood to milking goats.

But a stiffness, a decided reserve in her tone, mystified Gauk — until he stretched his arms down his sleeves and found that the tunic's shoulders were too tight and the sleeves too short.

"Please don't be angry," said the servant.

Her subservient tone, and the way she flinched when Gauk swung his arms, trying to loosen the cloth, made Gauk feel all the more self-conscious.

"I'm not at all angry," he said. "I am a little surprised that soaking in the spring has made me bigger than I was when I last wore this garment."

The servant put a hand to his sleeve. She said, "The laundry women were afraid the wool might shrink. And it has."

Courtesy was wise when a traveler inquired after someone's name, and so Gauk phrased his question using the time-honored phrase, "Whose daughter are you?"

"I am Jorunn Sursdottir," she said, "servant to Grim."

She was Gauk's age, he guessed, and her pale skin indicated that she spent little time outdoors.

"My clothes have shrunken only a very little," said Gauk. While it was true that the tunic was smaller, Gauk realized that the bloodstains were nearly gone.

"If you keep silent about this to my master," she said, "I'll find you a fresh tunic, of good lamb's wool, and new leggings as well."

"When I fasten my coat, no one will notice my long arms," said Gauk with a laugh.

"For your silence," she said, "I will do anything."

The warm spring purred and simmered behind him. Gauk considered what the comely Jorunn had just said. Sexual favors were often considered a part of a female servant's duties. Control over one's passions was admired as well as every other form of self-control, but Gauk felt a surge of temptation.

And a certain urgent curiosity. "Are you so afraid of Fat Grim?" he asked.

"No, not of him," she answered. "He is kind. His wife, however, is cruel," she added, lowering her eyes, "being jealous."

It was late in the day when Gauk followed the flowing shape of his own shadow up a wending, pebbled path to the seer's longhouse above town.

Now that he approached this heavily timbered dwelling, far from any neighbor, Gauk felt his steps falter. His newly washed clothes were not dry, after all. Gauk felt cold, chilled by the wind whistling across the long hillside. The steam from the hot springs up the rocky slope twisted and tattered in the breeze.

He wore the sword at his side, the best weapon he had found among the seamen he had killed. As he traveled the upward slope he fastened the ill-smelling length of hide and its dangling, black-clawed forepaw around his hips. If this offends the seer, thought Gauk, so be it. He wanted to hear the truth, no matter how painful. Gauk used Whale-Biter as a staff as he climbed the hill. He knew that he was a shabby figure, his wrists jutting from his shrunken sleeves within his shaggy coat.

He wished he had an excuse to turn back, but as he looked toward town he saw more than one person gazing up after him, each face as pale as a whalebone bead. One of the far-off observers was Jorunn, leaning on her laundry paddle.

She gave him a wave.

Twenty-four

In Spjothof a visitor announced his presence by slapping the door post and calling out. In other villages a whistle was considered proper. Gauk had heard of wealthy towns where knuckles were used on a door, but in Gauk's village this sort of knocking was considered impolite.

Ignorant of the habits of Blot, and apprehensive that the seer's servants would turn him away in any event, Gauk fell back on ancient formula. "The son of Ara," Gauk called, "humbly seeks to visit Jarn Ketilsson."

Impeccably polite though this was, it sounded unimpressive and even awkward sung out before a massive pine wood door. Beyond the seer's longhouse was the expanse of wind-stripped fields, white boulders, and distant forest.

Gauk called out again, until the door creaked open.

A giant of a man, sword at his hip, stood in the light of the late-day sun.

House karls were guards who protected the home and

the person of important men and women. Such men were not fighting men, as a rule, but that was largely because their very presence discouraged thieves and marauders.

This towering man with a flowing red beard had to duck his head to keep it from striking the door frame. He made no move to welcome Gauk. The hunter's voice was reduced to a croak, and the giant waited as Gauk cleared his throat.

"I will visit the seer," said Gauk, more assertively than he had intended. "If I may."

The guard gave a nod to the purse Gauk wore, all the silver fragments — broken plates and wine cups from far-off lands, and even a coin or two. Coins were rare this far north, and Gauk was pleased at the price the pelt had fetched from Fat Grim.

Gauk was all too aware that the pouch was not as plump as he could wish. He held out the pigskin bag.

The house karl poured the silver into his palm. The house guard did more than count the silver. He examined each piece carefully and with little haste, and Gauk quailed inwardly. Surely he had not brought enough.

The big man met Gauk's eyes with his own. The giant's gaze flickered down to the bear paws at his hip, and perhaps a trace of a smile creased his features for a moment.

Gauk kept himself from flinching as the giant's hand enclosed the top of Gauk's head and gave it a pat, the sort of caress a man gives a frightened boy. The huge stranger's eyes grew small with merriment.

Then the giant extended a long arm and pointed up the hill.

The horses were small, hairy steeds, still shedding their winter coats this far north. The animals bounded over the sun-gilded slush, five nearly grown colts the bright, pale color of birch wood.

A medium-sized man in a *kyrtill,* a hooded cloak, stood on the hoof-pocked hillside. He watched Gauk's approach. Odin was often depicted wearing such a hood, and the sight of this figure did nothing to hasten the young man's approach, or to make him feel less self-conscious.

Still, Gauk reasoned, there was no shame in needing advice. Stories told that the gods themselves sometimes cast lots or rattled ivory rune bones down on the forest floor to foresee who would win a battle.

To Gauk's surprise the man threw back his dark hood and smiled. This smile faded at once, and Gauk was aware of the pendulous weight of the bear relics swinging from his hip. Gauk bit his lip. He should have secreted the paws along the trail, but it was too late now. Besides, it was the pelt — and the life implied by wearing one — that had brought Gauk to this place.

The seer was missing the thumb on his left hand, but in a world of scars and old war wounds, this minor disfigurement was not remarkable. His eyes were as blue as any in Spjothof — neither eye was missing after all. His honey-bright hair was tied behind, in the manner of a seaman.

Jarn peered at the patches of gore stains still evident on Gauk's shaggy coat, and put a single finger on the pommel of Gauk's sword.

He walked an unhurried circle around Gauk.

Gauk's father had often remarked that any man could pass as a diviner if he collected evidence with his eyes and delivered prophecies that were sufficiently enigmatic. Indeed, there were many salty men of experience who scoffed at the power of such seers. And for just an instant Gauk wondered if he had squandered a purse of silver.

"You've been at sea," said the seer in a voice so gentle as to be nearly lost in the wind. He was a man neither young nor old, and his shy but level glance reminded Gauk of Errik the poet, a man who knew every chant and could invent new ones as lore-rich as the old.

And yet Jarn's remark demonstrated no unearthly power, Gauk realized. How else would a traveler arrive?

"I need your help," said Gauk, inwardly challenging this soft-voiced prophet to understand without being told.

Gauk blurted his tale quickly, not meeting Jarn's eyes. It

astonished the young hunter that words could encompass such events.

When Gauk was done, Jarn stood gazing down the hill, at the deep blue water of the harbor. It was late in the day, and fishermen were returning, their boats slow and heavy. Fishing was not an occupation that won particular glory, and while there were many poems about hunters and sailing ships, there were few stories about cod or herring, or the men who caught them. And yet the seer watched the fishing boats with interest, as though he had agreed to purchase the day's catch.

"You felt the bear-spirit possess you," said Jarn thought-fully, repeating this detail of Gauk's recitation.

"Yes," said Gauk, surprised that he still commanded speech.

"And you knew," said Jarn reflectively, like a man verify-ing the story he had just heard, "that you were stronger than any human warrior."

"Yes, I did!" said Gauk, grateful that Jarn understood.

Jarn said nothing for a long moment.

"You do not imagine," said the seer at last, "how many young men think that simply girdling their hips with a bear paw will make them a fearsome fighter."

Gauk chose silence.

"And you cannot guess," said Jarn, in an even voice, "how badly you offend me."

Before Gauk could protest, the seer turned and gave a long, sharp whistle.

At first Gauk thought Jarn was summoning one of the hairy, spirited horses. The creatures looked in Jarn's direction, their manes stirred by the wind.

Jarn whistled again, two fingers in his mouth.

The red-bearded giant appeared at the door of the longhouse. He made his way briskly, with huge strides, until he stood before Gauk and his master.

"Skall, this visitor has displeased me," said the seer.

The wind combed the giant's long red beard.

Jarn spoke quietly. "This fresh-faced young hunter styles himself a berserker, and believes Odin has chosen him."

Skall gave a silent laugh.

"Test him," said Jarn, "to see if it is so."

The giant drew his sword.

 Twenty-five

Gauk ducked the blade as it arced through the air and fell back, stumbling.

He thrust Whale-Biter toward the midsection of red-bearded Skall, but his towering assailant seized the weapon, wrenched it from Gauk's hands, and flung it far across the horse-cropped grass.

Gauk retreated, tugging at the sword in its scabbard. The weapon would not pull free. Skall took another slice out of the air, and only Gauk's nimbleness kept him from feeling a sharp edge cut into his limbs.

The horses scattered, snorting, kicking, losing a little more of what remained of their winter coats, the fine hair drifting, spinning in the softening wind. Jarn the Seer was a distant presence, huddled again in his hood, retreating from the violence. Gauk had tried to believe, for an instant, that this was all some rough game, the sort of manly sport that Norse folk loved. But as a blow hacked through Gauk's shaggy outer garment, the young hunter began to realize that the fight was in earnest. The steel kissed the flesh of his arm as Gauk rolled, tumbling, still trying to free his blade from its sheath.

Skall was on Gauk, the big man's fist seizing the younger man's coat. The giant dragged Gauk, kicking and still gripping the pommel of his stubborn sword. All the way up the hillside Gauk struggled, the seams of his coat ripping until the ground all around was sulfur yellow and the air was ripe with steam.

Skall dragged the younger man over the crusted yellow edge of the spring and plunged Gauk's head into the seething water.

Gauk felt the air explode from his lips, forced out of his body by the big man's weight. He lost all the feeling from his arms and legs, deaf to everything but the roiling, scalding spring. Gauk regretted, then, not putting his arms around Jorunn and telling her that he would take her away from this town. He regretted not praying more fervently for wisdom before he approached this place.

Even then he believed that Jarn would intervene, long before Gauk's head was boiled blind. He was sure this would all turn out to be a test, the sort warriors boast about surviving. Until he felt his body begin to die, he thought that Skall would laugh, and haul him dripping but still half-alive, the contest over.

Even now, all the air crushed from his body, the last bubble long since escaped from his lips, Gauk could think clearly. There was so much he wanted to tell his neighbors, Snorri's parents, the jarl and wide-eyed Astrid. He would never be able to tell the strong-armed Hego that the edge he put on a skinning knife was equal to the thickest hide.

And this made Gauk very angry.

The young man looked upward through the simmering water. Skall's red beard touched the hot spring, the giant's features glistening with the rising steam.

Gauk's hands awakened.

Help me, One-Eyed God, Gauk prayed wordlessly.

His hands groped their way upward, finding what they sought, losing, and finding again. They closed around the heavy beard, and drew the giant's head down into the seething water.

Blow by blow Gauk's fist punished the giant's features. Skall collapsed, rolling to one side, spluttering in the steam. Gauk climbed from the hot spring, and drew his sword.

He tasted blood.

He stood over a recumbent figure, the giant man with scarlet coursing down his features. Gauk was breathing hard, drinking the cold air in great gasps, swinging his head from one side to the other, scenting the air.

Twenty-six

Hego was searching, following the tracks of a sheep.

It was bitter cold in the predawn. He marveled at the way winter kept coming back, long after the ice had melted in the fjord. Hego breathed on his cold hands to give them feeling.

He was climbing high above Spjothof again. He loved these heights. It was so early in the morning the late-melting snow was glowing blue, the sun still hidden. The freezing air hurt his lungs, and the last of his ale headache was vanishing. There had been much deep drinking in Spjothof as men bound their wounds and cursed the Danes.

The sheep was stuck on a rocky ledge. At the sight of Hego toiling upward in the strengthening light, the animal let out a plaintive bleat.

"I see you," called Hego breathlessly, trying to sound reassuring.

He had awakened this early morning to the faraway, distant pleading of this stranded animal. It was more than compassion for this livestock that spurred Hego to climb in the darkness. The villagers had heard of Hego's battle with the Danes and expressed admiration, but it was not the praise they would have given a seasoned warrior. They were amazed he had not been killed.

The sheep was eager, now that a human being was approaching, and its anxious hooves danced so close to the edge. Hego had to close his eyes for a moment.

"I'm almost there," he called.

Gunnar had once told Hego that a sheep could not tell a boy from a goat. Hego could not imagine being so senseless. Nevertheless, Hego was puzzled at the curious nature of these ewes. Was a sheep stupid, or simply slow-witted and easily forgetful, like Hego himself? Why had only one of the breed ewes, driven into the high meadows the night of the attack, persisted in climbing all by itself higher and higher, until the echoes of its plaintive call were the only evidence that it was still alive?

He said, "I don't have far to go now."

Hego kept talking as he climbed, simply to give the sheep some hope, but he had to ask himself — what did a sheep think about? Even now, picking along the ledge from one vantage point over the precipice to the other, the ewe was in danger of falling, tumbling all the way down to the snowmelt-swollen streams.

Astrid had counted the breed ewes three times, and announced that one was missing. Old Gizzur had offered the opinion that one less sheep was of little consequence, but Hego was compelled by the belief that every lost sheep gathered in, every green timber planed and pegged to rebuild the ale hall, was another verse in the saga of Spjothof's recovery.

Hego knew the gods had spared his life, but he did not know why. He was stiff from the fall he had suffered, tumbling off the trail under the blows of the heavy-handed Danes, but he knew this accidental fall preserved him. A few more blade strokes and Hego would have taken a sword in the neck, or the chest, or in the skull, like the blow that had all but taken the life of the jarl.

Some half-intended slip of the Norns' hands as they wove the cloth of human destiny, some tiny thread floating one way or another, and Hego was healthy and the jarl was unconscious, oblivious to the quiet tears of his friends and his wife. Not three days had passed since the Danes had stolen Hallgerd, but no one had moved to seek ships for a mission to recapture her. It was true that just now Spjothof harbored only fishing boats and a few *sexeringr,* six-oared boats too small for a battle force. All the best fighting men were still off on a trading voyage, the most seaworthy warships absent with them. The village veterans had no choice but to wait. Soon *Landwaster* and her companion ships would stir the waters of the fjord, and then Thor, who loved just-revenge, would be their guide.

Hego reached the ledge, the gray-stone outcropping soiled with dung. The ewe bawled, even now, perhaps wondering why Hego had not clawed his way up the mountain with feed and water on his back.

"I'll carry you down, don't worry," said Hego with a laugh.

It would not be easy.

The ewe bleated right into his face, the sheep's breath white in the chilly dawn.

"You poor beast," said Hego, ruffling the animal's wool soothingly. "You're as stupid as I am."

As he flung the sheep over his back, high on the hillside, Hego saw the skip appear around the bend in the fjord.

The tiny, beautiful vessel was too distant for the creak of the oar locks or the stirring of the water to be heard, but Hego recognized *Strider*, its bare mast white against the shadows of the fjord.

One man in the boat. Only one.

Hego's breath caught.

Unless either Gauk or Snorri was hurt, or asleep, curled

in the prow. Perhaps the gods would heed the prayer of a fool with a sheep on his back. "Let them both be safe," he murmured.

Hego hurried. He slipped and nearly fell on the sloppy ice, the sheep over his shoulders enduring this means of transport with an empty-headed patience.

Hego reached firm footing, still high above the village.

He lifted his voice in the half-chant, half-wordless call the villagers had used since Thor's hammer was forged — the song of a vessel returning home.

Twenty-seven

Gauk smelled the charred timbers while he was on the water, far from the village.

Unexpected fires were common among the Norse, thatch and timber constantly proving treacherous. And yet Gauk stopped rowing for a few beats and drew Whale-Biter to his side. This was not a still-smoldering fire, he sensed. The conflagration was dead — three days old, he estimated, but the flames had been great enough that the scent still drifted down the sheltered waters of the fjord.

He did not smell death. He nosed the odor of wood ash, and the familiar smell of livestock and humanity. And something else — the very faint, earthy smell of trampled field grass and mud.

His oar strokes stirred the fjord's surface, and the widening ripples gently touched the cliff sides and spread outward again. The wake of *Strider* was quiet, the reflection of the soaring cliffs gently blurring, lost.

Facing aft as he rowed, the young hunter had to cease his effort and turn around to see the slowly approaching village. It was no surprise to observe that the warships were gone — their launching had been anticipated when he and Snorri began their own voyage. Gauk could make out what was unexpectedly missing — the gap among the village roofs where the ale house had stood. There had been a battle. Again he breathed the smell of foot-punished meadow and tried to believe that a large group of men had struggled for the sport of it, wooden swords against woven shields.

Gauk could see men and women hurrying from the houses at the sound of Hego's distantly echoing song — there was no mistaking that voice. Perhaps the villagers slackened a little when they perceived that the boat was the lowly *Strider,* and stood quietly as they recognized that Gauk was rowing in solitude. But cries greeted him then, Astrid's voice, and the granite-lunged Old Gizzur, the veteran villager, calling out encouragingly, "Well done, Gauk!"

A voyageur's return required a ritual.

Even now no one dared break the tradition of welcome and tidings that a hunter's homecoming demanded.

There was a moment of recognition when Gauk climbed from the skip. Eyes widened, and words faltered. All of them knew what his new white-pelted garment portended.

Gauk could not bring himself to tell the painful and disturbing events that had brought him this new bear garment. He had not even allowed his mind to fully consider some of them until now. The seer had given Gauk the splendid fur, one Jarn said had been left beside a sacred spring by Odin himself while the god took his ease in the warm waters. It was a luxurious pelt, fastened over one shoulder, and Gauk kept the sun-seasoned paws he had cut for himself dangling from his sword belt. The seer had explained that he doubted at first that Gauk was an initiate of Odin, suspicious of a young man's claim of divine power. Many men bragged, and young men boasted as well as the old. The fight with Skall had been the seer's way of testing the youth, and the wise man had intervened just in time to save the house karl's life.

But as to the young hunter's future, the seer had said only, "Odin gives, and Odin takes." It was this lack of promise, this failure to hear a word of reassurance, that had shaken Gauk so badly. Now Gauk's unhappy reverie was broken by a familiar voice, one that gave him joy.

"Is it Gauk?" asked his mother, helped down the rocky shore by her friends.

"Yes, indeed, it is," folk reassured her, "sound and happy."

The blind, soft-voiced woman did not trust the news until she felt his features with her hands and took him in her arms. "You are not hurt?" she asked.

Gauk laughed, to show her, and all his other friends, that he was healthy. But his voice was rough, his laugh ragged.

She hesitated. "You've come back bear-coated," she said, tension in her voice. To come wolf-pelted from a voyage meant that a traveler had met with honor in battle. To come back bear-pelted implied that the warrior had accepted a dangerous calling, one of long silences punctuated with battle frenzy.

Before he could say another word, she lifted her voice in a prayer of thanks to Freya, goddess of fertility and peace. This divinity, along with her brother Frey, was a provider of fertility and loving family life, peaceful endowments — compared with the double-edged gifts of Odin.

Twenty-eight

❖ ❖ ❖

Halfdan, Snorri's father, fought to keep from weeping.

A soapstone pot seethed on the hearth, giving forth the odor of boiled pork. Sometimes a family would roast a goose, or skewer beef on a stick, but pork and mutton were village staples.

Gauk sat at the family table and told the truth tale he had rehearsed in his mind. This, too, was a time-honored tradition, the surviving seamen delivering sad news to the families of their shipmates. Outside, neighbors had gathered respectfully, with a quiet murmur of voices.

Sometimes this sort of news was not accepted peacefully. Gauk told the truth, or as much of it as the young man could bring himself to recite. But it already sounded like a legend, Snorri a part of the past, drinking in the Slain Hall with the long-fallen heroes — as though his friend had been killed a century ago.

Katla, Snorri's mother, tearfully praised Gauk for his

friendship to her lost son. "You and he used to laugh so," she said. She told the story of the game they used to play, pulling a cow skull around the village. They used to pretend that they were Thor in the famous poem, trolling the deep for a whale, an ox head for bait. When they pretended a whale had surfaced, they had great sport dodging the flukes of the imaginary prey.

Gauk laughed sadly, tears in his eyes. For a moment he could hear his friend's laugh again.

"You'll drink with us," said Snorri's parents.

Gauk drank deeply of good, strong Spjothof ale, nothing equal to it in the world. The deep drinking was a necessary sign that Snorri's family welcomed him — and forgave him for surviving.

And then Gauk asked, "What happened here?"

Halfdan shook his head. Snorri's father was a cattle breeder, well known for the cheese his cows produced. The children of Spjothof were raised on cups of whey produced by Halfdan's herds. He was a short bull of a man himself, not given to speech, and gave a sorrowful snort in response to Gauk's repeated question.

"No one's willing to tell you yet?" said the mournful father at last. He wore a bandage around his right hand.

Spjotfolk did not like to give words to bad events. What

was said, and what was not said, could alter the subtle balance of things.

"If you and Snorri had been here," said Katla. "You and he would have stood proud and cut the Danes to the bone."

Astrid met him at the village edge, where the streams parted, heavy with run-off from the snowy peaks. This was another part of the homecoming tradition, the hunter washing in the rushing waters of Spjothof, drinking his fill and, in the streams that flowed from the hot springs, taking the first of several long, leisurely soaks in the warm water.

Gauk pulled off his boots and stood up to his knees, laughing in the rushing brook. The warm water felt wonderful, soaking into the wool of his tunic. Astrid was radiant, clinging to his hand as though he might be swept away.

He climbed back onto the bank, and Astrid, after a moment of reluctance, pressed her face into the rich plush of the white bear pelt.

"I asked the gods for dreams of you," she said.

"Did you see me shivering on the ice?" He wished his voice was not so hoarse.

She gave a gentle, troubled laugh, running her hands gently over the sun blisters on his brow, his lips. Her face was quick to color with emotion, and just now she was pale.

"I saw you clearly," she said, her voice broken.

"I'm going to talk to your father," he said.

Astrid's eyes were warm, but she said nothing.

"I'll tell him," Gauk continued, "that by the time barley harvest is in, I'll have your bride price."

"I saw you vividly in my dreams," she said, "and more than once."

Gauk wanted to speak about feasts and song, dancing, and the long years ahead. But he asked what Astrid had dreamed, fearing the answer. Odin teases with nightmares, Gauk knew. He probes human beings with lush images, feasting, laughter, and gratified desire, all the while holding off true fulfillment.

She did not want to put words to her dreams, but Gauk insisted.

"Birds were eating your body," she said.

Gauk's voice was a whisper. "You dreamed I was dead?"

"No, you were alive."

Gauk laughed, relieved. "And I am indeed!"

"Great black ravens were eating your body — and you were happy."

Gauk tried to laugh, the way Snorri would have, and make light of Odin's power to stir the psyche.

"Their black beaks," said Astrid, barely able to continue,

"plunged between your ribs, and plucked your eyes — and you were laughing."

"Tell me," said Gauk, when he could speak, "about the Danes."

She was the first to tell Gauk about Hallgerd, about the jarl's grievous injury, and about Hego's surprising courage and good luck.

The tidings filled Gauk with anger that was deep and cold.

Gauk and Astrid went to the place where pine planks were stacked, pegs already carved, ready to begin the rebuilding of the gutted ale hall. Within the warm welcome and the age-old requirements of homecoming, Gauk had perceived the sorrow. And something worse than sorrow.

Some emotion that Gauk could not name made the villagers' eyes downcast, their features shadowy.

Astrid lifted her voice in a saga lilt, the tone with which mournful or glorious tidings must be recited. Villagers gathered. Each man and woman fell silent as the beautiful young woman put her voice to the events no one else could bring themselves to describe. The beauty of the time-honored tune made it possible to put into words the painful events. Ordinary speech could not have borne the message.

"Are we certain who they were?" Gauk asked, looking around at the mourning ring of faces when Astrid was done.

No one could answer him.

"Do we know for a fact," Gauk persisted, "that these were Gudmund's men?"

Hrolf, the veteran warrior of legend, escorted Gauk to the door frame of Sword's-Rest, the jarl's longhouse.

Gauk was wearing his sword, and carrying Whale-Biter. The young hunter took the old fighter's arm as the door swung inward. "When are we sailing?" he asked.

Hrolf gave a sad smile, and to Gauk's surprise pretended not to understand what the younger man was asking. "Still wanting another hunt, after all your adventures?" said the house guard.

"When are we setting out after Hallgerd?" Gauk insisted.

"When the fighting men return again," said the veteran swordsman. "With ships and shields."

"But *we* are fighting men," said Gauk.

"And who'll defend the village when we leave?" queried Hrolf, "with every sword chasing south after an army?"

Despite the sound reasoning behind the seasoned warrior's query, Gauk recognized at last the character of the feeling that weighed down his old friends and neighbors.

It was shame.

Twenty-nine

A fire was snapping in the hearth, the smoke rising through the vent in the roof.

The firelight reflected off the features of the feverish jarl. Rognvald, Hallgerd's father, opened his eyes, but merely searched the roof timbers above. He beheld none of the reassuring faces bending over him. Fresh linen swathing around his head seeped blood. A Thor amulet, a silver hammer, was pinned on the blanket over his heart, and he wore a gleaming silver arm-ring to bring him strength.

"Gauk offers his respects," said Hrolf formally, emotion straining his voice as he gazed down at his master. "He is home from the ice."

The jarl parted his lips, his tongue darting, and he strained to raise his body from the pillows. No healthy man played host to another while lying on his back, but Gauk knelt and said, "Rest yourself, sir, I pray you," speaking as formally as possible. "I'll have an ale-worthy story to share when you are sound again."

Rognvald's hand found Gauk's. The great man's clasp was moist and weak. Even so, the proud jarl formed Gauk's name with his lips and made every effort to find the young man with his fever-clouded gaze.

The jarl lay under the finest blankets of woven wool. The family heirloom sword was at his side on the bedding — everyone knew that the battle with Death Herself was the only war that never ended. Even Thor had once wrestled Death, in the cave of the gods, and for all his divine strength he did little more than bring her panting to one knee.

In most Norse settlements the most capable physicians were women. Sigrid, the jarl's wife, and Fastivi, Lidsmod's mother, with her long blond and silver hair, were Spjothof's wisest healers. Everyone knew the story of how Odin had tested Fastivi years before, taking on the shape of a bear and slaying her husband. The young mother had to kill the bear with a thrust from her husband's spear.

Some towns had medicine women who received barley flour or wool cloth for attending injuries, a full-wound fee if bandages and ointment were required, bone payment for the loss of a bone or joint. In most settlements, the individual who caused the wound was responsible for the cost. In

Spjothof such medical help was given freely — the actual healing dependent on the mercy of the gods.

The jarl's wife accompanied Gauk to the threshold. She lingered there in the morning sun for all to see, letting the villagers recognize the respect she felt for him. The jarl and his wife had not hesitated to befriend Thorsten the berserker, although most of his other neighbors regarded him with great caution. Gauk was hopeful that the jarl's wife would acknowledge the new status his bear pelt implied, and offer him similar acceptance.

The usually talkative Sigrid was all but silent for the moment. Gauk, broken by what he had seen, could only offer his stammered, "The gods will not forget."

"Odin remembers," agreed the jarl's wife, laying a gentle hand on Gauk's arm.

Gauk flung a strong arm around Hego's shoulders.

"I thought of you and your whetstone out on the ice," and the young hunter.

"Surely not," Hego responded, blushing happily.

"You put such a fine edge on my blade, this one here," said Gauk, "that I could skin a bear as easy as —" He made an airy gesture.

Then Hego withdrew, suddenly aware now of Gauk's bear

fur garment, and the paws dangling from his belt. Even Hego, who gave little thought to his tunic or his leggings, could not misunderstand the stark implications of Gauk's bear garb.

"It's just me," said Gauk in a tone of forced reassurance. "The same as ever — very nearly."

Hego gave a nod of respect and uncertainty. Tufts of sheep's wool and a berry bramble were stuck to his sleeves, and his knees were muddy. "I spend my time tying and retying the knot around the sheep gate," said Hego. "And counting the animals, while you have been off having high adventures."

"You did battle with the Danes, from what I hear," Gauk offered. "You and Head-Splitter will find your way into a poem yet."

But Hego was quiet now, shrugging, not willing to compare his own fighting prowess with a berserker's.

"My new sword needs a better edge," said Gauk. He hated the way he sounded just then, his tone gruff, complaining. "I won it from a seaman, and I suppose there's tar on it. The thing won't draw cleanly from the scabbard," he added, sounding even worse.

Sea warriors often spoke in terse, wooden sentences, so manly they were above articulate speech. Gauk and Snorri had chuckled over this, but now Gauk's own voice had taken on the same self-serious tone.

"If you choose, I can knead oil into the leather," said

Hego, adopting the tone of helpful craftsman. "And cure the steel of any fault."

Gauk gave a nod, but felt a chill in his heart. He wanted to drink hard with Hego, and sing. Gauk did not enjoy the look of awe in Hego's glance.

Gauk dined with his mother, telling her an abbreviated version of his nights under the North Star.

It was good to be home. But the walls seemed to have closed in. The place was smaller than before. Her boiled lamb was as flavorful as ever nonetheless. He ate his fill, and then consumed more. He ate like one of the great-bellied men of legend, men who could devour an entire heifer at one evening meal.

He was dazzled at his good fortune, to breathe his mother's hearth smoke after such days and nights of danger, but his mother's anxious questions and the way her fingers searched out the sword nick in his shoulder, where Skall's blade had tasted flesh, made him wish he had not caused her such anxiety.

"If you had been here," she said, when she took away his empty wooden bowl at last, "you would have protected the jarl."

"How?"

"I know you could outfight any Dane," she said.

Gauk gave a laugh. "Danes use arrows and sling stones. In a sword fight, no doubt I'd have a good chance."

"Sword to sword, no Dane would be your equal."

His mother was not entirely blind. If she turned her head, and searched the light, there was a tiny remnant of vision, and she tried to find Gauk with her eyes now. He sat still, knowing that even when she glimpsed him he would be little more than a shadowy outline.

"Ara's son," she said, "would have defended his village."

"I certainly would have done my best."

Her next words both chilled Gauk, and gave him a deep thrill.

"That's why Odin has chosen you — and made you bear-pelted. To bring us back our pride."

Astrid's father, Horse-Trygg, met Gauk at the door to the family longhouse. In a breach of custom, he did not invite Gauk into the house.

Horse-Trygg was a well-known horse breeder, and so named to set him apart from Trygg Two-Nose, the warrior. The horseman walked Gauk up-slope to the horse pen of long black and white birch wood logs. Horse-Trygg was a small, stocky man, with a way of looking sideways as he spoke, cocking his head and emphasizing his slow speech.

He recounted a horse fight held earlier that summer,

with heavy wagers on both sides. Gauk had witnessed the fight — the entire village had, but it was typical of Astrid's father to recount an event as though he had been the sole witness. Gorm, one of the horse owners, had cheated shamefully, wounding the opposing steed with a blade.

"It hurt my heart," said Horse-Trygg with a sigh, "to see a fine little fighting horse disabled like that."

Astrid's father held out a fistful of toasted barley, and his horses, frisky, short-legged creatures the color of soot on snow, nosed their way forward.

"I owe Astrid my thanks," said Gauk, "for telling me so frankly what the Danes have done here."

"Astrid is a clear-headed young woman," said Horse-Trygg. While not a fighter, Horse-Trygg's success in breeding and training animals had given him a certain honor, and he spoke like a man who expected his words to carry weight.

"No other neighbor would tell me," said Gauk.

"Bad luck," said Horse-Trygg, caressing the nose of one of the horses, "clings to the mouth."

"I want to speak further with Astrid," said Gauk.

"Of course you do," said Horse-Trygg. "All those days out on the ice and sea, and you want to look into a pair of blue eyes and tell your story."

Something about the man's tone stung Gauk. "And I want to speak with you."

"What about?" asked Horse-Trygg, not meeting Gauk's eyes.

"I'll have a bride price in my purse," he said. "By the end of summer."

"How will you get that, Gauk?" asked Horse-Trygg, digging into his feed pouch for more toasted grain.

"By the labor of my back," said Gauk. "Planing logs and chopping wood."

"Ah, Gauk," said Horse-Trygg in a tone of regret — even sadness.

The horses chewed, their working jaws crunching the grain. Horse-Trygg massaged the ear of a young mare.

"I did, at one time," Horse-Trygg continued, "think of you as a young man with years ahead of you. I always liked you. But now —"

He let his eyes linger over the bear belt fastened at Gauk's shoulder. Many men had a grudging admiration for the fighting reputation of the berserkers, while acknowledging that such men were little more than devotees of the sword, lacking in the quiet steadfastness respected among the Norse.

"Now," said Astrid's father, "I am not so sure."

Thirty

Hego's household ale was thick as soup, with a thick yellow head. He could consume the stuff by the cupful, but he was a little embarrassed to serve it to a visitor.

Gauk drained his drinking horn, a receptacle that had been made from the polished, sweeping horn of a great ox many years ago. The horn stood on little legs of a metal nearly as bright as silver. Hego's drinking horn had belonged to a distant uncle, a man who had traveled east as far as a land where archers rode horses backward and people played a game consisting of driving a goat's body from one end of a field to the other. The horn was far from being an object of dwarf craft, but it was the most expensive heirloom Hego owned.

Hego's ale was brewed by his servant Jofridr, who made a point of keeping the recipe secret. "My husband Rurik liked ale you could spoon out," Jofridr was saying. "He said ale was like bread but better for the heart."

Gauk had swallowed his share of the brew. He was perched on the edge of Hego's tool bench, among the shears and ax heads people had left for the blade smith to sharpen. Hego and Gauk agreed courteously with the long-dead shipmate, and lifted their cups to him.

Jofridr crossed her arms, cleaning rag folded and tucked in her apron. The evening was cold, and yet in here the fire was merry. "Rurik was a real man," she said. "With warm blood and hot breath."

"We all raise our cups once more to honor his memory," said Hego, a polite phrase he knew was appropriate whenever the dead were mentioned by name. This could go on all night, the dead honored by ale drinking until no one could speak or stand.

"We have our memories of better times," said Jofridr, tears in her eyes.

Sometimes Hego could not follow Jofridr's train of thought, and he wished he was not in such a dull-witted frame of mind. He had worked cow's foot oil into Gauk's sword sheath. Hego did not think much of the scabbard's leather work. Some squint-eyed craftsman had stitched the horse leather with awl and rawhide, and the result was a scabbard the blade slipped into with a difficulty matched only by the strength it took to wrest it free. It was much better now.

"My Rurik," Jofridr continued, "was not like the half-men we have around the village today."

"I'm sure not," said Gauk, meeting Hego's eyes.

While women were never law speakers and female servants were relied upon for years of uncomplaining labor, it was not uncommon for these valued family retainers to have many worthy opinions.

"You hear what he says, Hego?" said Jofridr.

"What does he say?" Hego asked, weary affection in his voice.

"Your friend agrees that we are a town of spiritless men," she said.

Sometimes conversation got Hego into trouble. This was why he liked the company of ewes and breed boars. "Yes, that's what we are," said Hego, sure, even as he spoke, that agreeing with Jofridr was not a good idea.

"You see?" said Jofridr, stirring the hearth embers. "We all know it. Only a berserker has any courage in this town, and everyone knows a berserker is worse than a drunk."

Cold are the counsels of women. It was an old proverb.

Gauk climbed down from his perch on the workbench. He whisked the sword from its scabbard and replaced it, taking a fighting stance a few times to test the leather.

"So now you are ready for an enemy," said Hego.

"If I ever set eyes on one," Gauk agreed.

To Hego's surprise Jofridr burst into tears. "Who is to keep us alive in our beds," she said, "with only fools to guard us? And which of you will be man enough to bring Hallgerd home?"

Hego could not sleep. Sometimes ale made him drowsy, other times it quickened his pulse and filled him with visions.

Jofridr was snoring. She had drunk her fill of her own ale, and when she spoke in her sleep she uttered names of the honored long dead.

Just as he was about to drift off, Hego heard something. The sound was far away, and very quiet.

Two booted feet stirred the pebbles of the shore. The mares were silent, and the breed ewes did not stir. If the Danes had come again, the animals would have sounded an alarm, and the recently posted sentries would have raised a cry.

Hego rose. The moon had risen, a splinter of blue light slipping under Hego's door. He found Head-Splitter beside his bed.

A keel makes an unmistakable grating noise, as it is guided over the rounded pebbles of the shore — even a small craft, shoved gently along, in an effort to muffle the sound.

*　　*　　*

It was dark.

The moans of the people still hurting from the Danish attack, and the soft murmurs of the people who attended them, were audible throughout Spjothof.

A few guards had been posted, noted Hego, but the veterans were set to guard the mountain passes. Only two sentries defended the fjord. Old Gizzur was slumped beside the wharf, asleep. A young boy, Thorfinn — son of an expert carver — gripped a spear, gazing out at the dark fjord.

Someone had run *Strider* out into the cold water, the disturbed water lapping faintly at the pebbles along the edge of the fjord. This obscure figure was busy in the prow of the boat.

Hego turned to the young sentry and put a finger to his lips.

Hego held Head-Splitter high, keeping the keen blade dry. He waded nearly all the way to the vessel before Gauk looked up from the provisions he was arranging and said, in a whisper that carried through the silence, "No!"

Hego hurried through the shockingly cold water.

Gauk continued to speak in whispers that echoed softly throughout the fjord. "Stay home, Hego!"

Hego covered the remaining distance, swimming with strong strokes, the battle-ax held clear of the water.

"If you come with me, you'll never see Spjothof again," Gauk said, looking down over the side of the skip.

"I'll fight at your side, and die singing," said Hego, treading water and shivering. It was an old phrase, taken from some half-remembered saga.

"I'm going to rescue Hallgerd," said Gauk in a quiet, determined voice. "And if I can't, it doesn't matter. Who cares if a berserker lives or dies?"

"Please," pleaded Hego, "help me out of the water."

Thirty-one

Hallgerd stepped into the light of the fire, her eyes smarting from the smoke, and waited for her hostess to speak again.

The woman was in no hurry to do so, but at last she broke her silence. "Hallgerd, from the brave village of Spjothof," she said, her pale, finely woven gown rustling as she moved. "I am honored to meet you at last."

The woman plunged the glowing end of the hardwood staff into a drinking cup at her feet. It was a method used to warm a drink quickly and to spice it with hardwood, a flavor some people enjoyed. The beverage sizzled.

"All along the north coast," said Hallgerd, with what she hoped was proud courtesy, "people honor the name of Arnbjorg, Gudmund's daughter." Her father and mother would have been pleased at the courteous firmness of her voice, but Hallgerd hoped her hands did not tremble as she accepted the drink from her hostess.

Arnbjorg was an amber-haired woman, and the cloth of her dress was beautiful, like the white of the moon — undyed wool, Hallgerd guessed, of an unusual breed of sheep. The sleeves of the dress were fastened with pretty knots. Not only was the garment attractive, it also demonstrated that the wearer had servants to fasten the sleeves. No one in Spjothof had taken up the style.

Syrpa, standing well out of earshot, kept a bright gaze on Hallgerd, with an unspoken plea: *Don't betray my confidence.*

"I am glad to see," the noblewoman said, "that you are as beautiful as the reports of men portrayed you."

Hallgerd was determined to make no further remark until she could quiet her pounding heart.

But the woman's eyes were amused, as though sure that a young woman from a farming village would not know how to speak well. Hallgerd responded in customary phrases, offering respect to the house that had sheltered her for the night. Then she added, trying to sound sure of herself, "I insist that I return home at once."

"Let's have our day meal first, shall we?" said Arnbjorg, using the familiar word *dagverdr*, the same one used by Spjotfolk for the food eaten at daybreak. "And before we eat, drink some of your mead and take a walk with me — I have something to show you."

Arnbjorg reached out, and Hallgerd flinched.

It was an involuntary start, and she hated herself for not seeming calm.

Arnbjorg gave a quiet laugh. "You have spirit. Snebjorn will be a lucky husband."

She followed her hostess out the timbered doorway, into the cool morning.

She was grateful to be outdoors again. And Hallgerd wished she could set eyes on Thrand once more — she missed his reassuring glance and his gentle voice. At the same time she suspected that escape down one of these shadowy, crooked lanes would take her to freedom. But which one?

A thin-faced servant came with them, stepping softly behind. Eaves overhung the street, and barrows of raw wool and flax were awaiting entrance into many of the houses. Doors were opening, and yawning, puffy-eyed inhabitants smiled curiously at Hallgerd as she passed. Many of the lintels and door frames were elaborately carved blade work that Hallgerd was forced to admit to herself was capable work.

Alrek the berserker greeted her from an open doorway. He was fastening his sword belt, his hair and beard mussed, his bear pelt askew. A woman's voice behind Alrek chided him to close the door against the chill. Hallgerd noted to herself with interest that among the Danes it seemed that even the berserkers had wives or *frillur* — concubines. In many villages along the north coast berserkers had trouble winning the company of women. More than one account told of a berserker who killed a woman while in the transports of bear fury, an act considered shameful.

Hallgerd admired the timbered walls they passed, carved in places with decorations, serpents and ships. She paused at a smoothly hewn ladder. "Can I see the view from up above?" she asked.

Her hostess smiled, but made no remark.

"We have no such walls in my village," Hallgerd continued, truthfully enough. It was also true that anyone from Spjothof would find such walls confining, preferring the clean, uninterrupted wind off the fjord.

"You'll never see such a fortress, if you traveled to the edge of the sea," said Arnbjorg. "My father's walls are like nothing ever built."

They kept on and did not stop, past a tanner hanging out his hides, the air nearby redolent with the pungent smell of the curing vat and the stench of untreated animal skins. The tanner was complaining to a thrall, and the thrall kept his rough-wool hood over his head. In Spjothof, tanning was carried out by farmsteads, just like brewing and cloth making, and there were no professional leather merchants.

A bucket of tallow, used in dressing leather and making

candles, sat outside a butcher's shop, and in the open shop of a smith the nearly dead coals awaited the arrival of the craftsman and his bellows. Blacksmiths were rare among the Norse, iron being hard to come by. Such a shop, Hallgerd realized, was further evidence of this town's wealth.

They came into the shadow of a dwelling so new that sap seeped from its timbers. Even before she approached the threshold she scented it, the building smelling of freshly cut timber and sawdust. Hallgerd did not want to see this place. The door was so new that the blond wood grain caught the early morning sun, gleaming. The roof overhead was shingled with stone — an unheard of extravagance in Spjothof, where turf and wood were the best anyone could afford.

"After my father has returned," said Arnbjorg, "and the wedding preparations are complete, this will be your home."

Every step and murmur echoed off the empty walls.

The construction was green pine, the roof posts still seeping subtle beads of sap. The house was like many great houses Hallgerd had seen, the roof beam massive, crossties supporting the weight of the roof. But no building in Spjothof was as grand as this.

In addition to several storage rooms, the house boasted a new feature, one unknown to her — an inner space, open to sky, encircled by the house itself. "It's a courtyard," said Arnbjorg. "Frankish traders have told me that such spaces are prized among the people of the south."

"All the better to keep me prisoner," said Hallgerd. Nevertheless, the beauty of the building stirred her.

"I knew," said Arnbjorg, "that you would prove a woman of great will. I am considered a woman of spirit, too." There was a tone of hope in Arnbjorg's voice as she added, "We will learn to enjoy each other's company, don't you think?"

Hallgerd was ashamed she could not make any progress in the contest of wills between Arnbjorg and herself. Every alehouse sported talking contests, proving who could invent the best poem, or remember the most ancient songs. But it surprised Hallgerd that her hostess had sounded just a little needful for a moment, as though she might enjoy the company of a jarl's daughter, even one years younger and from a northern village.

Her hostess was continuing, "King Sigfred of the Danes has asked my father to fortify this coast. Charles the Great, the king of the Franks, wars against the Saxons, these Saxons spill into our kingdom — so much is unsettled. My father is off supervising the building of walls up and down our kingdom. Gudmund needs an alliance with brave people. With your village in particular. It will buy us peace."

"Peace, but not friendship," said Hallgerd.

"My father wants to protect the Danish kingdom," said Arnbjorg, "from a repetition of that blood-soaked summer when your Spjotmen harried us so badly. I told my father that my plan was wise, adventurous, and that it would work. To unite the men of your brave village with us, you will marry into my family."

Hallgerd was familiar with the political reasoning behind such marriages, but she felt the breath leave her body as she understood how helpless she was. "My father will have no trouble finding Gudmund's stronghold, and burning this place to ash." Hallgerd knew this could well be an empty boast.

She was nearly as tall as Arnbjorg, and Hallgerd estimated her own strength, and how long it would take to strangle the noblewoman with her naked hands.

"I have spoken with my cousin Thrand," continued Arnbjorg. "He told me every detail of the attack on your village, and how bravely your neighbors fought." Arnbjorg looked up at the great hole in the roof, where the hearth smoke would rise up into the sky.

Hallgerd made no further response. She was aware that Arnbjorg looked directly at her when she added, "I believe your father will not object to the marriage when he considers the treasures we will offer him in return."

Her hostess tugged the door of a storage room, and indicated well-woven cloths already stored there, folded on the shelves, each blue-and-red fabric the result of the finest loom craft. Furs were there, too, examples Hallgerd had rarely seen before — martin, she guessed, as well as fox and sable. This was going to be a handsome house, the home of a wealthy woman. Many stolen brides would accept their position as one of unexpected good fortune.

Hallgerd reflected once again on the fact that kings and jarls could seize a bride as booty, and that this marriage was considered both binding, and a possible source of material advantage for the bride and her village. A forced marriage was often long and fruitful, once rich payment had soothed the offense. Lidsmod was a keen-eyed, good-tempered young man, respected by all, but her father had yet to fully consent to the marriage between the youth and Hallgerd.

Marriages were arranged by fathers, and where two countries and complex politics were involved, Hallgerd had heard of a *mundr* — bride price — of entire shiploads of cows or horses. Even though his voyage to the west had been successful, Lidsmod would have trouble raising a price that could compete with the means of this wealthy Danish family.

As she stood in the emptiness of this nearly completed dwelling, Hallgerd realized the temptation even a protective and loving father would feel in having his daughter so well married, with a satisfying bride price delivered in shiploads.

"If my father arrives and agrees to the marriage —" Hallgerd began, her voice sounding weak.

She nearly added, *I may accept it.* But the memory of Lidsmod's voice, and his touch, silenced her.

"And if your father does not arrive," said Arnbjorg, "will that not be a sure sign of his assent?"

Hallgerd recalled then Olaf's voice, murmuring confidingly beyond her locked door last night. She had almost been able to make out the words. Now she was beginning to guess what he had been saying.

Thirty-two

Olaf had been boasting, sharing a secret. One of the servant women had prompted him, keen with questions.

Hallgerd probed her memory, gazing up at the blue sky above the fireplace. As she watched, a raven appeared, a glinting, blue-black pair of wings.

Hallgerd, the raven cried, an utterance that sprang not from the bird's black beak but from within Hallgerd's blood.

Two more times it seemed to intone her name. The bird settled on the new, bare timbers of the roof, and looked directly into Hallgerd's eyes.

Many folk dreaded the possibility that an animal might have discourse with them. But some highborn families had a tradition of accepting wisdom from animals. As a girl, Hallgerd's mother had once heard a distant buck elk bugle the name of her grandfather, and the famous, white-bearded old man had not awakened the next dawn.

Now this handsome raven parted its beak and gave a cheerless laugh. *Hallgerd — trust her not.*

This was a fragment of high speech, the way gods and heroes spoke in the sagas. Hallgerd was speechless, both fearful and rapt at this message that came at the raven's prompting from within her own heart.

Arnbjorg was oblivious, describing the number of thralls that would supply the house with its needs.

Hallgerd gazed upward, unable to move or make a sound. There was no sure protocol for receiving word from the far-seeing god. Hallgerd soundlessly shaped the question, gazing at the great bird, "What can I do?"

The divine messenger had red eyes, unlike the black eyes of an ordinary raven. The black apparition parted its beak. And when Hallgerd heard the voice again, as before, it did not seem to come from the raven's black tongue, but from within her own breath.

Believe nothing, Jarl's Daughter.

Hallgerd was silent, praying that the winged apparition would say more.

But the bird shook itself, all its feathers awry for an instant, and then winged away, its flight making a rustling, rhythmic whisper. And it was then that Hallgerd began to guess what Olaf had been saying — that the jarl was not unhurt.

That the Danes had left him bleeding on the ground.

Arnbjorg was describing the cloths that would hang on the walls, scarlet and blue. Gudmund's daughter had heard nothing out of the ordinary, it seemed, nothing more than one of the town's ravens croaking.

Hallgerd exercised the greatest self-control. She managed to give her hostess a smile and said, when she was able to make any sound at all, "The seamen of this town are nearly as accomplished as the men of my village."

Arnbjorg accepted this compliment with a nod.

"My neighbors make strong oarsmen," said Hallgerd, "but they splash the water, and spill ale on each other, and by the time they reach port they look like they've been painted with pitch."

Arnbjorg gave a gentle laugh. "We are proud of our sailing men."

Hallgerd could not suppress the thought that Arnbjorg was far too proud altogether. She continued: "I wish you would allow me to visit Thrand. I would like to thank him for bringing me here safely."

Arnbjorg turned to look at Hallgerd — surprised at the younger woman's sudden graciousness, or perhaps suspicious. "Thrand knows all the coastal soundings from Freylief to Nidaros," said Arnbjorg with an air of quiet superiority. "By heart."

Hallgerd knew that this was a pointless boast. Any man or woman in Spjothof could recite the route up and down the coast, and most of the children, too. But Hallgerd was pleased that she had correctly judged the degree of her hostess's pride.

"Does he indeed!" said Hallgerd. "You must allow me to express my gratitude to your noble cousin."

To her surprise, Arnbjorg gave a laugh that was almost friendly. "I do believe that you've captured Thrand's heart, Jarl's Daughter. My cousin speaks of nothing but your great poise during the voyage, your dignity, and your spirit. And, I think, he did mention something of your beauty."

Hallgerd wondered at the sweep of feelings that rose over her. Was it possible that she blushed?

Her hostess sent the thin, quiet servant who had shadowed them off to locate her cousin, and Hallgerd's heart quickened in anticipation.

Perhaps buoyed by pride in her own town, Arnbjorg allowed Hallgerd to climb one of the timbered walls.

The town of Freylief was on a peninsula of bog land, inlets slicing across the gray-green wetland to the east. In the distance a birch forest stood, a wall of shadow.

Hallgerd took all this in from her perch on the fortification, memorizing as much as she could of the byways and moorings. It surprised her that there was no bottom to her hostess's vanity. No compliment was too great — the citizens were handsomer, their wood smoke more fragrant, the slop buckets in the streets less noisome, than those of any other town.

Small boats nestled among the earthwork fortifications on the landward side of the settlement, where the scything watercourses cut across the wetland. The tide was low, and these stranded boats lolled lopsidedly in the mud. A child and her mother wandered the grassy earthwork, stopping to gather what, at this distance, looked like shellfish. A net mender had spread his morning task on the shoreline and was beginning to tie knots in what gave every appearance of being an ancient fishnet.

The town was bustling. Somewhere a bellows was working, smoke rising from a smith where a metal worker's hammer was making its *ping-ping-ping*. Geese quarreled, and a cart rumbled through a muddy lane. Hallgerd climbed down again, until she stood at the foot of the timber wall.

Thrand hurried along a lane. For a moment Hallgerd was very glad to see the seaman again, and this feeling of welcome did not surprise her. After all, he had been a source of reassurance during the voyage here, and she believed that Thrand had some warm regard for her. Surely he smiled now that he stood before her, and he looked directly into her eyes. Was it possible? she wondered. Had Thrand lied about her father's well-being?

His tunic was smudged with ship's tar — he had evidently been summoned in the middle of overseeing the re-caulking of *Bison,* but his face and hands were pink with recent scrubbing. "I trust that our town's hospitality pleases you," said Thrand.

"It is hard for an imprisoned woman to say," rejoined Hallgerd, "what will please her, and what will not."

Thrand put out his hand and touched her arm reassuringly. "I hope," he said, "you will be happy."

"Tell our guest," Arnbjorg was saying, "how many planks it takes to build one of our household ships." She said *karfi,* the word for a jarl's vessel, lovely but rarely used in warfare.

Thrand took a moment, glancing from Hallgerd to the busy lane beside them. He did not look directly into his cousin's eye as he said, "They have many seaworthy ships in Spjothof."

"But nothing compared with ours," suggested Arnbjorg in an almost hopeful tone.

"My father will look forward to inspecting your shipyard," said Hallgerd. "When the decks are soaked in Freylief blood."

Hallgerd was ready to breathe into Thrand's ear, *Please tell me again that my father is unhurt.* She stepped close to him while Arnbjorg was busily describing Freylief's earliest origins, generations ago, when a village of shellfish gatherers arrived and began draining wetland.

Thrand must have guessed the question in her eyes. He inclined his head toward her and whispered, "Be patient." There was something further he was about to tell her, but he hesitated.

"Do speak up, Thrand," said Gudmund's daughter, "so I can hear you, too."

Just then a song rang out — and another. Clear-voiced calls rose from several points throughout the town.

They followed the throngs toward the harbor.

Four warships approached, oars flashing. The arriving crowd of townsfolk began a chant. The pulsing roar was meaningless for a long moment, but then it shaped into unmistakable, joyful syllables as men and women gathered to greet the ships. *Gudmund.*

The name was echoed by a hundred voices.

Later Hallgerd would wonder if she was surprised at the cheers that greeted the famous war chief. Cruel though he might be to his enemies, women held children high so they could see his ships stirring the black water of the harbor.

Arnbjorg hurried Hallgerd back into the hall, and posted a double guard at the young captive's door.

Hallgerd listened as what she assumed were mead barrels rumbled across the hall, and thrall and servant alike scurried, pushing tables and benches into place.

Syrpa entered the chamber and looked on as serving women arranged small white flowers in Hallgerd's hair, the tiny blossoms Spjotfolk called Meadow's Breath. "Speak only when Gudmund asks you a question," said the housekeeper.

"I know how to speak to a jarl," said Hallgerd. She tried to sound brave, but her voice nearly failed her.

"No, please forgive me, I doubt that you do," said Syrpa. "Gudmund is the killer of many men. And you'll be meeting your intended husband this evening, if you receive Gudmund's approval."

"Then I hope Gudmund loathes me."

The housekeeper stepped back and surveyed Hallgerd. "You will win the heart of anyone who meets you," said Syrpa. "Even that great slayer of enemies."

The young woman dreaded the forthcoming encounter, but would not let anxiety enter her eyes. "Is it possible," said Hallgerd as servants tied her sleeves, "that you could tell the noble Gudmund that his captive is ill, and that she begs that she could see him some other evening?"

"Gudmund will see you tonight," said Syrpa, "if I have to drag your corpse across the floor."

Thirty-three

Hallgerd waited in her chamber as the sounds of laughter and song drifted from the hall. The smell of roasted pork and goose reached her, too. Despite her uneasiness, she was hungry.

Mead cups clanked and chants were recited. From where she waited, secluded in her chamber, she could make out the fine voice of a poet, and a passage of high-verse.

> *Seas we sailed, iron-fisted,*
> *spears and shields bloody.*
> *The wolf-coated, the bear-clad,*
> *fell away in fear.*

She recalled the poem well, one of hundreds that celebrated battle. She knew the chant would go on to recount the courage of a young woman named Thora, who fought off an army so her brother's spear-slain body could be carried home.

Hallgerd sat on a stool, her fine-wool skirt flowing across the floor. Surely they will forget all about me, she thought as the song came to an end accompanied by cheers. They will drink and play games, she reassured herself. And then they will fall asleep.

This hope kept her heart from pounding.

A time came, however, when the song and laughter ebbed. A voice was lifted in speech, the sound of a woman. Arnbjorg's voice did not carry well through the timbered walls, but the young captive could not mistake what was being said.

The syllables of her own name.

Syrpa hurried into the chamber, mouthing, *Come quickly.*

Hallgerd was already on her feet. If the Song of Thora gave these Danes spirit, it gave Hallgerd herself exactly the same courage. And more.

She left her chamber, and entered the smoky, fire-lit hall.

The hearth smoke was thick, and the benches crowded, faces flushed with feasting.

A man wearing dark blue wool and a silver arm-ring rose

as she passed. At first Hallgerd thought this red-bearded man might be the man she was expected to marry. But then she noted the piece of hack silver beside the man's mead cup, and realized that the man was the *skald,* the poet with the pleasing voice. He had just been awarded a piece of war booty — seafaring warriors broke silver dishes into pieces so they could be easily shared.

Poets were as well honored as any warrior among the Norse, and held with an apprehensive respect by many people — they could weave a song extolling a man's skill, or mocking his judgment. "Your voice is a gift," said Hallgerd, pausing at the poet's bench, "that brings Odin pride."

A murmur ran through the crowded hall, a tone of approval at her courtesy. Then the folk were hushed, intent on what the poet would say in return. Even the thralls, most of them garbed in light gray or blue tunics as they served the teeming banquet hall, fell silent. Olaf paused, a drinking cup halfway to his lips, and Thrand, seated on a nearby bench, gave Hallgerd a smile of encouragement.

The poet gave a bow. "Just as your beauty, my lady," he said, his fine voice uplifted, so all could hear, "gives pride to man and god."

This was met with whispered admiration for both poet and prisoner. Arnbjorg took Hallgerd's hand. Her touch was dry and cold as she accompanied Hallgerd to a place before the high seat at the end of the hall. But Arnbjorg's pulse was quick, her breath fast, Hallgerd could sense. As confident as her hostess could seem, she was apprehensive regarding her father.

Gudmund was white-haired, his locks flowing over his leather-clad shoulders. His nose had been broken at some point in the past, a common injury in an age when combat was hand-to-hand, the bronze boss in a shield's center doing damage where sword work failed. His garments were the shining, flowing fabric Hallgerd had come to recognize, a tunic of sea-blue silk.

The famous warrior turned and allowed a servant to pour mead into his silver cup. He thanked the server in a low voice, and when he turned to face Hallgerd he took time to savor his drink before he lifted his eyes to hers.

"My father's daughter," she said, "thanks you for your hospitality."

Gudmund wiped his white mustache with the knuckles of his right hand — his sword hand, deeply carved with scars.

His eyes were measuring, but not unkind. The trace of a smile slowly softened his sun-weathered features. Hallgerd recognized this steady gaze, and it troubled her. She had expected to hate — if not fear — Gudmund, but something about his bearing reminded the young woman of her father.

The legendary sea chief did not speak, and while his countenance was welcoming, he had no intention of trading greetings with her. It was usual for a jarl to measure his silence carefully, and Hallgerd was not offended.

Gudmund gave Arnbjorg a long glance up and down, and made a circling motion with his hand.

"My father wants you to turn around," said Arnbjorg.

Hallgerd did as she was told, resenting the bloodshot eyes and the mead-wet lips of the warriors around her. She would obey the great war jarl — she had no choice. But she felt a simmering dislike for this hall of curious eyes. She turned all the way around once, until she faced the white-haired man again. But as she did so she took in the expressions of the faces around her, and realized something she had never understood about herself before.

She had been pleased the way her long hair flowed down her shoulders as she looked out of her father's windows, and proud of her clear voice when she sang, and her strong stride when she ran. But not until now did it fully impress her that she was beautiful — enough to make her the talk of distant towns.

Gudmund gave a nod. He lifted one finger, and a young man stepped forward from the haze of wood smoke.

The youth introduced himself — Snebjorg Adillson,

"whose father lost his life against the Franks two summers past." He wore a fine wool tunic, earth-colored, and his appearance was neither pleasing nor displeasing. He was not at all like Lidsmod, whose eyes were always quick, his face alive with feeling. If Lidsmod had been a boat he would have been a quick-sailing craft, with a sharp keel. This young man was like a freight ship — steady, unexciting. But he gazed at her with a warmth — even a pleasure — that could not be mistaken.

The Danish youth Hallgerd was intended to marry continued to speak of himself in the third person, as was proper, saying that his father's son was pleased to offer her shelter and safe harbor. These were customary phrases, and once again Hallgerd recognized that, despite her captive status, the folk of this place were treating her with elaborate courtesy.

She turned to the jarl himself. "Wise Gudmund, I seek your permission to ask a question."

The legendary warrior lifted his silver cup, and for a while it was as if she had not spoken. Then, before he took another sip, he lifted one eyebrow in assent.

"Tell me, Gudmund," said Hallgerd, choosing her words with care, "on your honor — does my father still live?"

Thengskapr.

That was the word for honor Hallgerd used, and she chose it carefully. She was asking for Gudmund's word as a nobleman.

The old jarl put both hands on the arms of his oak chair. With the assistance of a spearman, he got to his feet. He stood swaying, whether from infirmity or an excess of mead, the young captive could not tell. A guard steadied him as he made his way toward Hallgerd.

Gudmund stood before her and ran his scarred hand over her hair. Was there, she wondered, an air of sorrow in his countenance? She was aware that she could have seized a sword from a nearby guardsman's hilt, and run the old man through. But she did nothing while the legendary sea chief put his hand on her shoulder.

He patted her, as a man might console a nervous animal. Or, perhaps, a bereaved daughter. Gudmund turned back to his high seat. The great fighter sat with difficulty, and took his mead cup in hand once again without uttering a word to his captive.

Thirty-four

She sat in her chamber once again, her heart racing.

The guard at Hallgerd's door was joining in the singing, raising his voice with all the others in a rousing, tuneful song about a ship so gracefully constructed that the oarsmen rowed across the sky.

A footstep whispered at her door. Thrand stood in her chamber, putting a finger to his lips.

Hallgerd had been weeping, but she quickly blotted her tears on her sleeves.

"At least bloody-handed Gudmund would not deceive me," said Hallgerd. "As some seamen have."

"You asked Gudmund to confirm something impossible," said Thrand, his voice barely above a whisper. "How can even he say who lives or who dies, four days' sail across the sea?"

"Was my father," he asked, choosing her words with care, "in sound health when the Danes left Spjothof?"

Thrand lifted his hands in protest. "I was not with the band who confronted your father's sword."

"But you know what happened."

Thrand ran his gaze over the floor.

"You've known all along," said Hallgerd. "I heard Olaf boasting about it — words it took me a long while to understand."

Thrand turned away from her.

"All your men knew," Hallgerd said, pacing, unable to stand still. "The message was in their eyes, but I could not read it — or did not want to."

Thrand did not speak.

"Tell me," said Hallgerd, barely able to control her voice, "how my father died."

"He was alive when we left him."

Her eyes spoke for her. *I don't believe you.*

"But he had suffered a wound at Odd's hands," Thrand continued reluctantly, "a sword cut to the head."

Hallgerd felt her throat close, the pulse frozen in her body.

She had hoped that she was wrong. She had prayed all along that she had mistaken the signs all around her.

Then her faith stirred again. "But he was still alive!" It was a statement, not a question.

Thrand bowed his head. "He was."

"Give me a satchel of food and a skin of water. I'll escape this place and begin my voyage home tonight."

Thrand made a helpless gesture.

"My father will hear of your kindness, before the gods," said Hallgerd, resorting to the finest speech she knew. "And I'll pray my neighbors to spare your life."

Thrand did not respond.

"Some bread," said Hallgerd, "and water. Nothing more."

Thrand parted his lips to protest.

Hallgerd continued, "I don't ask for a ship or a ship's boat — or even a hollow log and a paddle. I'll choose my own sea craft. I ask only provisions — and one more thing. One thing I think you can give me without risking your life, courageous Thrand." She could not keep the sarcasm from her voice.

"My severed head on a stick?" said Thrand with a pained laugh.

"A homespun cloak, with a hood."

"Hallgerd, I expected you to be a young woman of fire, and beauty. But I did not expect to feel as I do."

The emotion in his voice surprised Hallgerd.

"I regret having had a hand in your sorrow," he said.

Hallgerd could not suppress a moment of affection for this gray-eyed Dane.

"But you won't be able to flee Gudmund," Thrand was

saying. "Men obey him because they have no choice." The seaman stepped to the game board and picked up one of the soapstone carvings and very gently put it back again. "I am not a weak man, with Thor's help, but Gudmund and his daughter can be unforgiving, even to a member of their family. We sail, we utter lies, we draw blood, all because it pleases Gudmund."

What moved Hallgerd she could not have said. She rose and stepped to Thrand and put her hand on his shoulder — just as Gudmund had touched her.

"You will help me, friend Thrand," she said in a low voice.

Thrand's eyes were bright with feeling, but he did not assent.

She added, "Before the gods, I ask you — please."

The feast was at its peak, talking contests as every table, bragging contests, story games, testing who could tell the best story, the most fearsome, the most scandalous. There was a traditional game in which the virtues of a person or beast were enumerated, until the list had gone on so long that men who were sober when the game began were slurring drunk at its conclusion.

It was not the first time Hallgerd had felt a tug of kinship among these Danes. The hall was a riot of boisterous song and dancing. Men and women were entranced with each other's company, embracing, leading one another off into the shadows. Gleeful figures cavorted near the hearth fire, and thrall and guard alike joined in the singing, a song Hallgerd did not know, about a mare who wished a stallion would stop breeding with the clouds and come back to earth where he belonged.

Hallgerd was hooded and cloaked, her fine gown with the knotted sleeves left behind. She was swift in following Thrand, who was garbed in similar fashion. Arnbjorg was singing, along with everyone else, her eyes ablaze with mead and the obvious relief that her father had returned from sea safely once again. Hallgerd and Thrand walked quickly, looking, Hallgerd prayed, like two slaves hurrying off to attend to some household emergency.

Only one person was aware of Hallgerd and Thrand, watching through the thick feast smoke.

As Thrand opened the door and stepped out into the darkness, Hallgerd glanced back to survey the room.

Syrpa's eyes caught hers.

Thirty-five

Hallgerd followed Thrand through the muddy, crooked lanes. The town was quiet, except for the roaring, cheering tumult from the hall, and that chanting grew increasingly distant. When Thrand stopped and pressed against a wall to look back and listen, Hallgerd followed his example.

The door of the newly constructed house was unlatched, and swung inward. The rooms echoed around them, each footstep resounding in her prospective home. Starlight fell through the hole in the roof, where hearth smoke would someday rise.

The door to the storage room was so new, it had no latch, swinging silently on its hinges. In the almost total darkness it took a few heartbeats for Hallgerd's eyes to adjust to the shapes of things around her, shelves and the woven baskets that would be used to store grain.

"Perhaps she did not know who we were," concluded

Hallgerd, giving a brief account of their departure from the hall.

"Syrpa knows everything that happens within her walls," said Thrand.

"She was kind to me," said Hallgerd.

"Syrpa was working hard to impress you," said the seaman. "She believes that someday Arnbjorg will be gray and toothless, and you'll be a power here. Still, she's not a heartless woman."

"I pray she is not."

"I'll speak with her," he said meaningfully. "Look at this grand house!" he added in a tone of wonderment. "Arnbjorg and her father made glorious plans for you."

An alarm rang, far off.

Many towns had a warning iron, a metal rod that hung from a crosspiece. Such irons were rung to stir a town against attackers, or to warn of some all-consuming emergency. Now an alarm rang ceaselessly, some brute with a powerful arm striking it, and then pausing only to change hands and continue ringing. Voices joined in, cries and shouted commands, the words indistinguishable but urgent. It seemed to Hallgerd that she heard the far-off sound of her own name.

"How much danger," asked Hallgerd, "have I put you in?"

"No great risk, Jarl's Daughter," said Thrand with a quiet laugh. "And even if you have — I've tasted danger before."

"My village will pay any price you ask, if you take me home." There was a vague, moonlit gleam about the place, the plank floors dimly reflecting starlight from the courtyard.

"Every ship will be searched, every sea chest," said Thrand. "Hide here, Hallgerd, in this storage room. If Arnbjorg's house guards search this place, get into one of these new curd vats and pull the lid over you. No one will expect you to be hiding here in this house — they'll be searching the boats."

He was speaking quickly now. "I'll send word to you when it's safe to leave, and I'll bring you food." He retreated, his silhouette dim in the doorway.

Hallgerd tried to shape some high-speech farewell, but approaching steps that splashed puddles in the streets outside silenced her for a moment.

"Go," she urged, "before they find you."

He did something then that surprised Hallgerd, and moved her deeply. He returned through the darkness, took her hand, and kissed it.

And then he was gone.

Armed men searched the house the following noon.

Hallgerd had awakened to find a satchel of bread, a wedge of golden butter, and a clay bottle of water. Now the empty building thundered with heavy footsteps, men dragging their spears, in a hurry as they barged into the shadows. In the pine-scented rooms the scent of the spearmen was ripe, sweat and ale, the urgent odor of men in trouble, the way rowers perspire when a ship runs aground.

Hallgerd faded from room to room, just ahead of them, until she crawled into one of the curd vats and curled inside. The container smelled of newly cut wood, and the lid fit snugly over the top. The total darkness nearly choked her. She held her breath as big feet paced the storage room beyond, heavy strides echoing off the wooden walls.

If the searchers had said something it would not have been so bad, just a few syllables so she could judge them, and understand how desperate or angry or weary they might be. But there was only the scuffling of feet, and the sigh of someone slamming the storage door, shutting it again, and giving up when it didn't latch.

Arnbjorg searched the house herself the following night.

She was accompanied by a serving woman and two armed men who stopped at the threshold, as though Hallgerd, flushed like a rabbit, might escape out the door. The servant carried a candle, their shadows huge across the bare floor.

Hallgerd slipped into the storage room, once again climbed into the wooden container, and crouched there, her eyes shut tight. She knew that any moment the noble-woman's hand would seize the lid, snatch it away, and empty Hallgerd out onto the floor.

Gudmund's daughter wept. These were not tears of sadness but frustration and anger. Arnbjorg pounded on the timbers supporting the roof. She kicked doors shut, flung them open. And then she said, "Give me the candle."

The servant was silent.

"Can you smell her?" demanded Arnbjorg.

"Lady Arnbjorg," stammered the servant, "I cannot tell."

"I can nose her well."

Hallgerd knew where Arnbjorg was, following her with her mind's eye every moment, the noblewoman pacing, pausing, pacing again. At last Gudmund's daughter gave a wall a kick and called out, "Where are you, farm girl? Come out or I'll burn these walls down around you."

Hallgerd's body gave a quiet, inner murmur. Barely a sound at all, and certainly inaudible beyond the vat.

"I heard her just now," said Arnbjorg. "Didn't you?"

The servant was in apparent agony, admitting that she had heard nothing. "She's far north by now, I believe, Lady Arnbjorg — on the sea."

"She would rather freeze on the gray ocean, you believe?" said Arnbjorg in a tone of thorough skepticism. "I don't think anyone is so foolish."

She entered the storage room. Hallgerd saw the faintest glimmer of candlelight where the lid — that had always fit so well until just now — had settled crookedly over the opening.

Arnbjorg stood there for a long time, while Hallgerd held her breath.

And then she left without a further word.

Thirty-six

Hallgerd was not accustomed to solitude.

No one in Spjothof was ever alone indoors. The quiet insistence of the loom shuttle, the grinding of barley in stone querns, the sweeping, the washing — it was all fueled by conversation. All the day's work was accompanied by song, and laughter, and gossip.

She slept and woke. She waited — when had she ever had a life of color and cool wind? She could not remember it clearly anymore. She chewed the shrinking crust of bread and hoarded the last sips of water. The wind sang overhead, along the stone shingles of the longhouse.

The ravens called, but they sounded like mere birds now, scolding each other, greeting each other — or laughing.

*   *   *

When she heard a door creak, and a tread in the room outside, one part of her mind no longer cared if the visitor was captor or friend.

A familiar voice called her name.

Syrpa carried a satchel, and she knelt in the half-dark of the big house. Hallgerd left the shadows to meet her, grateful at the sight of another human being.

The housekeeper gave an account of what was inside the bag, wheat bread and dried cod, and butter. "With this much food you could sail from here to the North Star," said Syrpa.

There was indeed a pleasing weight of provisions in the satchel, enough for one person sailing four days.

"You'll find water in the boat I've prepared for you," said the housekeeper.

"You didn't bring me a weapon, Syrpa."

"What sort of blade would have pleased you?" said Syrpa. "A harpoon, maybe, so you could run men through — the way you've managed to skewer Thrand."

Hallgerd began to have some understanding of Syrpa's feelings toward Thrand, and the skein of jealousy and loyalty that tugged at the capable woman. Hallgerd said, "You have been kind to me, Syrpa, from the beginning."

"My dear lady, when I first saw you I thought that

Thrand had captured a very pretty shepherd's wench. Your garments were of coarse herringbone weave, if you'll forgive me. Only when you spoke did I realize that, by Thor and the north wind, they had brought back the woman of good name they had been ordered to capture. There will be a sleek little boat moored in the harbor." She used the word *pramr*, a compact little craft used for transportation from wharf to ship. "There you'll find a seal spear and some fishhooks in the vessel. Most of the ships are off searching for you." Syrpa paused, waiting for her to give a sign that she understood.

Hallgerd did understand, but was too thrilled and hopeful to do more than nod.

"Take the boat to sea," said Syrpa, adding a few directions through the lanes, down to the moorings. "Not just now — a north wind is blowing. But when you hear the wind shift, make all haste."

"You are a loyal friend," said Hallgerd.

"You are a good-hearted woman, Jarl's Daughter," said Syrpa, "and I mean you no harm, but Arnbjorg could lock you in a cage and I would do little more than pity you. Thrand convinced me to do this, and my heart is weak. I don't know why I heed the counsels of men, especially a well-made nobleman with gray eyes."

"Syrpa, you've treated me well, and I am grateful."

Syrpa looked away, as though stubbornly trying to deny her own kind nature. "We owe our peace to Gudmund," she said, "but some of us have little love for his daughter. Besides, she played a dangerous sport when she captured you. The forced wedding would only be acceptable to Spjothof if your neighbors and family were largely unharmed." The housekeeper spoke formally, but with warm feeling in her voice.

Syrpa turned back once before she left. She had something further to say, a final message. But whether it was blessing or warning, she said nothing more. Her footsteps padded across the timbers, and she was gone.

Thirty-seven

The north wind died, and the house was quiet.

Hallgerd left in the darkness. She felt exposed under the starry sky, certain that someone would spy her and call out.

She did not seek the byways down to the harbor — not just yet. She walked quickly, hidden in the homespun hood, the leather pouch of provisions on her back. Hallgerd made a mistake, turning into a broad street where two men were talking, laughing, rattling dice. Spearmen consulted with each other at the end of this lane, and down another a guard clambered heavily up the wooden stairs to the top of the wall, calling out a greeting to the watch he was relieving.

Freylief was restless on this summer night, every shadowy shape Hallgerd glimpsed sporting a shield and spear. A voice called out, "Thyri, do you have my jug?"

Hallgerd shrank into the shadowy angle of a building, praying that the guard had not seen her.

Alrek the berserker trudged forward along the lane.

"Thyri," he called again, using a feminine name common among the Norse. He came closer. He stopped in his tracks only a few strides from where Hallgerd stood, her form pressed against the hard pine timbers of the house.

"Thyri, I'm thirsty," called the big man.

He came even closer, the leather of his boots creaking. With muffled chime he withdrew his sword.

Hallgerd could see him clearly now, the starlight gleaming off the bear claws around his neck and the long shadowy blade in his hand. She smelled the sweet waft of mead on his breath, and marveled at the town-broken nature of these people. Even a berserker was reduced to half-drunken guard duty here, no more menacing than a haystack. At the same time she well remembered the lessons every child in Spjothof learns, the violent sport of disarming an opponent. She would hurt him, if she had to, and take the sword from his hand — as Thor gave her strength.

Alrek knelt. He nearly toppled over as he probed a mouse hole across the lane with his blade. He sang a childhood ditty, one Hallgerd remembered from her childhood: *Wee friend come out, I mean no harm.*

"Put your sword in its sheath, Alrek," said Hallgerd in her best version of a Danish accent. "Find some useful thing to do, instead of hunting mice."

"Ah, so I will," said Alrek, straightening with a start and

doing as he was told. But peering around, too, even as he returned his weapon to its sheath.

Hallgerd brushed by him. She hurried off down the lane, from shadow to darker shadow, and she sensed Alrek's mead-heavy wonder. Whose authoritative voice was that? Some housekeeper, was the impression Hallgerd had sought to make — some woman of high character few men would happily debate.

"Ingigerd?" he called doubtfully from behind her, and then, trying out yet another name, called, "Gudrun?"

She walked with the deliberate gait of a townswoman as long as she could control herself, and then at last she ran. She shrank back into a dark lane, and followed another route. And, for a few moment, she lost her way, and had to double back.

Hallgerd nearly stumbled on a bucket of tallow outside the butcher's shop, even though it was exactly where she had expected it to be. She knelt and pressed her finger on the yielding, ivory pale fat. This was excellent tallow, the sort collected from the kidneys and livers of fatted livestock. She gathered up the bucket, the weight swinging easily in her grasp.

Hallgerd stole quickly into the smith's open shop. The metalworker's hearth was all but dead, the tongs and hammer hanging on hooks. She used a pair of tongs to probe the ashes, reaching deep, until she brought out a barely glowing ember. Hallgerd breathed on the faded coal, and it came to life.

She entered the new house once more, carrying her burdens easily. Hallgerd took the tallow and the coal into the storage room that had been her sanctuary. She eased the block of tallow out of its bucket. The pale fat kept the shape of its former container, and Hallgerd placed the flickering coal on top of the liquid. A flame started, blue and shivering.

That was all it took — a darting, transparent feather of fire, and a spill of tallow, trickling down to the floor, flames blossoming. The storage room began to fill with the tallow smoke, and the smell of burning pine.

Hallgerd crept down the face of the earthen embankment, on the marsh side of town. Syrpa's directions proved more than helpful. The boats there floated listlessly, tied to moorings that angled one way or another, the air ripe with the smell of decaying wood and brackish water, peat and fresh night wind. Already there was another smell, the scent of green timbers burning.

The boat she chose had a mast stretched out in the hull, and a pair of oars, white in the starlight. The vessel felt alive under her weight, but she groped about and could not find a seal spear, and certainly no fishhooks pricked her touch. She was in the wrong boat.

This was an unpleasant discovery. But before she could continue her search for another vessel, something about the small vessel's quickness under her weight, and its balance, reassured her.

The oars slipped in and out of the dark water. They were so noisy! A cry lifted through the starlight, half-alarm, half-question.

Hallgerd gave a wave, and the guard began to return the gesture — and hesitated. He called out a challenge, and she began to row in earnest as, over the peaked roofs of the town, flames burnished the sky.

The alarm was sounding, faster and more urgent than before.

Thirty-eight

Hego was thrilled.

Strider sliced the sea swells. The black waves fell away behind them, and he and Gauk took turns at the steering oar.
Hego laughed at the way the seabirds dodged out of their
way. A sole gull flew alongside *Strider,* showing off the
strength of its wings, but at last even this stalwart bird gradually lost the pace and fell behind. Hego gave a cry of de-
light, waving his sea-soaked cap in triumph at the retreating
bird, and Gauk had to laugh, too, buoyed by Hego's high
spirits.

The sailboat was what the folk of Spjothof called a stiff
vessel — she remained well balanced no matter how hard
the wind blew. Hego knew as much as any Spjotman about
small craft. Many times he had rowed a ship's boat yelling
and whooping, driving a whale onto shore where the beast
could be harpooned and flensed.

"I didn't know *Strider* was so fast!" cried Hego.

"Odin guides us," said Gauk in a matter-of-fact tone.

Hego had always trusted the divine powers to provide fair weather and strong ale, and he had never hesitated to lift a song in prayer or thanksgiving. But a god had never given him a message, or taken an essential role in the young man's life. Having heard Gauk's tale of the bear and the taunting pirates, Hego was awestruck.

"No man will be able to stand against us!" Hego exclaimed.

"I hope you're right," said Gauk.

"I'll be your shipmate from the salt caves to the serpent's mouth," said Hego. It was an old phrase, implying tireless loyalty.

Gauk gave a sad smile. "Snorri used to tell me that."

Hego was impressed beyond words by the transformation that had come over Gauk. The young hunter's eyes had depth now, and his words had more weight than ever before. At the same time, Hego had heard enough about killing pirates. Hego sought a saga-worthy adventure, culminating in the rescue of Hallgerd. It would be as well if no lives were lost.

When the boat hit a ridge of submerged stone along the coast, Hego took to the oars, timing his effort to the arrival of a large wave. The craft rose high up the wall of water, soaring even higher, nearly dumping the two young seamen.

But then the prow fell forward, the craft slipped gracefully down the back of the wave, and they left the boiling surf behind.

Hego's heart quickened as they approached the shallow bay where the town of Akerri nestled, one of the southernmost moorings in Norway. Gauk had explained that they would find provisions here, for a price. Hego knew this town was famous for its bullies and its cheese, and the young man was a little apprehensive about visiting the place.

Akerri was an old word that meant anchor. Gauk suggested that *Cutthroat* would be a more appropriate name, from what they'd heard. *Strider* found a place among a few shabby shore boats, and nosed up along the sandy shore beside the quiet water.

"I'll go into town myself," insisted Hego. "I'll bring back a cheese as big as this." He made a great circle with his arms. "You guard the boat."

Gauk hesitated, his eyes alive with concern for his friend's safety. "I don't want to offend you, Hego. But be careful. These townsfolk are wicked sly — I've heard there's no end to their trickery."

Before Hego could respond, a voice interrupted the two.

A burly guard carrying a long spear and wearing an embroidered wool tunic called out, "You two, in the boat."

Hego gave what he hoped was a friendly smile — there was no use in antagonizing anyone unnecessarily.

"It costs you a toll, either cloth or fishhooks, to beach your keel here." The guard had a square jaw, big yellow teeth, and hugely muscled arms and legs.

The spearman took a long look at Guak's bear pelt and Hego's ax before he added, more politely, "That's the custom here, if you'll forgive me."

Gauk murmured, with a world-weary smile, "The trickery begins right here!" He gave Hego a handful of delicately carved bone craftwork, fishhooks and thread makers. All these objects were decorated with fine details only the skilled folk of Spjothof could produce, and represented a degree of portable wealth.

Hego knew better than to offer more than he had to, and paid only a deer bone needle, a choice piece of work, which the guard accepted with a grudging wrinkle of his nose.

"Call out for me, Hego," said Gauk, "if there is the least danger."

Cutthroat, thought Hego as he strode toward town. Wicked sly.

Surely the town's ill repute was exaggerated.

The path to the settlement was long, pocked with puddles, and lined on either side with windswept shrubs. A small creature, a field mouse or a vole, darted into its tunnel as Hego passed, and the young blade smith chuckled with a show of false ease, a manly sort of laugh that pleased his ear.

He tried it out again, a good laugh. Hego kept a carefree smile on his face, and strode along with studied confidence. He didn't blame the tiny creature for seeking shelter.

He reached the edge of the village.

One bald-headed man flung open the door of a long-house and stepped into the sunlight. He put his hands in the pockets of his apron and eyed Hego as the young traveler approached.

"We have no cheese here, seaman," said the man in response to the young traveler's request.

Hego was very hungry, especially now that he could smell the ferment of cream and the brewing of ale from the longhouses scattered around the village. Eyes peered from doorways, and Hego tried to look agreeable.

And he struggled to look confident. He carried Head-Splitter in his belt, the ax-head at his hip, and he put his hand on the sharp-edged weapon — casually, as though his hand naturally rested there.

The aproned villager added evenly, "The cows have just now been herded up to the meadow where they can feed on green grass."

"They've been eating grain, and you've been milking

them all winter," said Hego, puzzling through what the villager was telling him.

"Old dried-up hay is what they've been digesting," said the aproned man. "We've had snow on the high meadows until just this week. Ask anyone and they'll assure you Cow-Bjorn knows curds from water."

Hego could not hide his disappointment. Furthermore, he suspected the man was lying. Surely the cattle had been able to graze long before now.

"They call me Cow-Bjorn for good reason," said the man, whose face had the open, intelligent look of a trustworthy villager. "I know how to keep thunder from curdling cream. Believe me, sailing man — every wheel of cheese in this town has been eaten up by hungry women and children, many months ago."

Hego gazed at the ground, dazed with disappointment.

Cow-Bjorn sighed regretfully. "I do wish I could help a traveler in need. Especially a young man from Spjothof, where the women weave that fine herringbone cloth, and the carvers are legendary."

Hego took a handful of finely wrought bone fishhooks and beads from the inner pouch of his tunic.

"Good seaman," said Cow-Bjorn, "you don't realize how costly nourishment can be."

Thirty-nine

Hego's pouch was empty, but he carried a great cheese at the end of a stout stick.

The cheese was heavy — it was like carrying an axle attached to a wheel made of food. Cow-Bjorn had sworn it was the last edible cow's cheese in the village, and had wiped a tear at the thought of the children who, he said, would have "wrinkled little bellies because you've taken the only real nourishment."

He hurried along the path to the beach. The wind-battered shrubs on either side of the path shook and trembled, and more than once Hego paused to listen. He could make out what sounded like muttered curses, and the whisper of a knife withdrawn from a leather scabbard.

Hego hastened forward.

When two men in ragged gray wool leaped into the muddy path, and a pair of arms hugged him from behind, he was not totally unprepared. It was a ploy associated with disreputable villages — sell provisions dear, and then steal them right back again.

The young Spjotman shrugged his shoulders and sent the assailant on his back crashing into a puddle. The two youths in the path ahead crouched, holding their knives the way men in alehouse brawls were known to do — blades loose in their grips, ready to slash.

Hego struck the taller of the two with the heavy cheese, and the youth went down hard. The remaining attacker lunged, and suffered a blow to the temple, followed by another. Hego belabored his attacker with the cheese until the youth sprawled, covering his head and calling out for help.

The remaining youth scampered from his puddle and was running fast toward town.

Gauk hurried from the boat.

"This is a village of rank shorerakers," said Hego, using the derogatory term for landsmen. "*Cutthroat* is too good a name for this place."

"You aren't hurt?"

"Thor protected me," said Hego. "Thor, and his great hammer of cheese."

Gauk laughed hard at this.

Hego did not know why they didn't take advantage of the ebbing tide at once, row out into the current, and leave this place far behind. But Gauk saw no need for speed. He produced his skinning knife and sawed the cheese's tough rind. Hego urged him to hurry, but his companion was deliberate.

As Gauk worked, several men appeared on the beach from the direction of the village, walking in the stiff-legged, theatrical manner of folk expecting trouble. Gauk handed Hego a wedge of cheese.

One of the band, a broad, hairy man with eyebrows growing together in the middle of his face, trudged down to watch them feast.

It was the finest cheese Hego had ever eaten.

The hairy man was wearing a sword, but as he eyed the two Spjotmen he made no move to draw his weapon. "Cow-Bjorn knows nothing," said the hairy townsman at last. "That's how he earned his name — for his cow-like stupidity."

Hego was finished trading words with the people of this place. Gauk spat a bit of rind and shrugged, as if to say: *What message have you come to deliver?*

"My name is Ox-Onund, and I can sell you five more cheeses just like that one," he said. "But much better."

"If we wanted more cheese, we'd take it," said Gauk. "And spare your lives, if we felt so disposed."

Gauk spoke amiably enough, but he gave just enough

emphasis to his words to impress Hego, who began to wonder just how capable in battle his friend might prove to be.

"We'd be grateful if you spared our lives," said the hairy man, with an unruffled air that belied his words. "Dead men eat very little in the way of cheese."

This brought a quiet laugh from Gauk. "For a price we will leave your village unpillaged, your women intact, and sail away."

The group of men had fanned out along the beach, one or two of them collecting stones, a few of them resting their hands on their sword pommels. These were heavyset men, with thick legs and heavily muscled arms, the fathers or older brothers of Hego's assailants. A few carried shields, and several brandished wood-axes.

"Name a price," said Ox-Onund evenly.

"The sword at your belt," said Gauk.

Hego knew that some warriors sailed to seaside villages and extorted valuables from the town's elders in exchange for leaving the village unscathed. He had never met an outlaw so reckless, and had never dreamed he would be in a position of sailing with one.

Or pretending to be one himself.

Ox-Onund snorted, thought for a while, and smoothed out a rough place in the sand. "This sword is the product of dwarf craft, found by my grandfather on a glacier."

Gauk pared another portion of cheese and chewed for a while.

"This pommel is silver, marked all over with magic runes," said Ox-Onund. "If you plunge this blade into a river, a floating leaf will part around the blade, cut in two — it's that keen."

Gauk chewed and swallowed.

"So the price you ask," added Ox-Onund, folding his arms, "is too high."

"My friend Hego will cut the legs off your neighbors," said Gauk, "before he roasts the poor folk alive."

Hego understood now the sport Gauk was playing. A battle boast was an ironic form of courtesy — the more outrageous the threat, the less likely it was to be carried out, and yet the more obviously impressive your opponent was made out to be. After an interlude of swapped boasts, both sides could retire in dignity.

Hego tried to ready a boast of his own. He tried to assume the grim expression he imagined such a boast would require, if he was required to make it, but it was hard to look brutally self-assured while eating cheese.

"I think," said Ox-Onund, "that my friends and I will teach you a lesson in hospitality."

Later, Hego would puzzle through what happened next, making sure he kept the order of events clear in his mind.

A breathy whistle cut the sky high above. A thin shadow plummeted from the blue. With a splintering crash a spear quivered in the planks of *Strider.*

When an Odin initiate hurled a spear over the heads of the enemy, it consigned his opponents to death. A townsman Hego had not yet encountered now hulked down the sandy beach. He was, by all appearances, a berserker.

Every trace of false bravado vanished within Hego. This was a big man, taller and beefier than Gauk. His bear pelt was soiled, trailing in tatters past his knees. Two bear paws dangled from his belt, and black claws gleamed on a cord around his neck. His fellow townsmen cheered the berserker's arrival. Others followed, young and old, a small army of spectators.

"Yngvar Vemundsson!" called Ox-Onund theatrically. "Come and help me with our visitors."

The pelt-clad warrior descended the slope, drawing his sword.

Forty

Gauk was surprised, but not, as yet, very concerned.

He had not expected to confront another Odin initiate, it was true, and he was unprepared for what might follow. But the big man had only two arms and two legs, Gauk reminded himself, and Odin rewarded the cunning.

Hego gave Gauk a worried glance, but the young blade smith was a Spjotman and would not panic. Gauk offered his friend a brief, reassuring smile. Later, when he had time to reflect, Gauk would realize that this was where he made his mistake.

I should have been praying, Gauk would think. Instead, I was putting on a demonstration of unconcern, pretending that I had invented courage. My cockiness offended the gods.

Yngvar parted his lips in what might have been a grin or a grimace. The sound of the big man's laughter reached Gauk's ears — full-chested, boastful laughter — followed by a bear-like roar. The big stranger put on a demonstration of berserker mannerisms, shaking his beard, spit flying. He raised his eyes skyward, invoking the divine.

Hand-to-hand combat had a protocol. A terrified man sang a war song to conquer his fear. Some lyrics mocked the opponent. Others praised the pedigree of the weapon being drawn from its scabbard, usually an heirloom associated with many years of lore. Gauk responded with an attempt at an ursine bellow of his own.

But he forgot to pray. Immediately he was struck by a deep unease. His sound was fake and without power, even to his own ears, a falsetto shriek, lost in the ocean air.

When he tried to roar once again, his voice failing, a sick doubt swept Gauk. He went cold, and his muscles went slack. Too late, he tried to whisper a prayer to the One-Eyed God, but the words would not come.

The fight was already lost.

The armed spectators jeered, observing Gauk's weakening spirit, marking his fading courage. These shoremen had the look of seasoned fighters, scarred and deep-chested. They'd seen many men die bleeding. They pointed at Gauk, and laughed. One man let out a breathy scream in mockery of Gauk's bear yelp.

"Odin be my strength," the young berserker rasped.

Far, far too late — the god had chosen sides.

Gauk shrank inwardly. Odin did not have to be fair. Capricious, even fickle, he gave — and he took away.

As the bearded berserker closed in on Gauk, the young man did not feel his courage quicken. He felt no electric anticipation as he found the pommel of his sword and drew his weapon. Gauk realized that he had tarried too long on this shore, and misjudged his own strength. Now he was as good as dead.

Snorri would have told him as much. Bad sleep, troubled dreams, and days of sailing had made him weak and worse — he was careless. And soon to be humiliated.

Hego pulled Head-Splitter from his belt, but Gauk put a hand on his companion's arm.

"There's no use both of us dying," said Gauk. "Get into the boat."

Tradition and good sense called for a fighting verse. Hego began the first words of such a song, one of Spjothof's favorites, Thor climbing the mountain over Spjothof to seize the handle of his great hammer.

A gull overhead laughed, a long, mocking *ha!* Waves tumbled, weakened by the ebbing tide.

Gauk dies, whispered the winking foam.

Odin, the All-Seeing, gave power and, when he chose, he took it away again. The god knew much, and a young hunter like Gauk knew nothing. He took a deep breath, and let it go.

So be it.

Hego's song had a certain power to it, and for the moment it gave Gauk the inner fire he needed. The young berserker had no particular fear for his own life, but he regretted bringing Hego to an early demise on this worthless beach.

The big bear-clad warrior warmed up his sword arm with a few passes in the sunny air. Yngvar's weapon was huge, and decorated with runes. Such magic made a weapon even more deadly.

Gauk positioned his own body between the big berserker and Hego, who continued to sing with increasing vigor. Yngvar had left a set of footprints all the way down from the dry sand to the wet, and now, far from acting out an uncontrollable frenzy, the big man took some time to smooth out the sand. He flicked a piece of driftwood with his boot, clearing a flat fighting space.

Gauk made an effort to portray the same confident, pre-fight ritual the veteran berserker did, kicking a pebble out of the way, shrugging to loosen his shoulders. The spectators doubled over, laughing.

Yes, thought Gauk, there is much to mock — if only they knew.

Yngvar strode down toward the younger man, showing his many teeth in an ugly smile. The big berserker's first assault was an overhead swing, easy to see coming. Gauk fended it off with the flat of his blade — it was important to keep the edge of his weapon from being hacked ragged by the heavier sword.

Block, parry, feint — Gauk performed well for a few moments.

Yngvar stepped back, repositioned his feet, and cut a wide, sweeping arc, with no apparent attempt to catch Gauk off-guard. Yngvar's blade was surprisingly fast, however. Gauk leaped back to keep the point from slicing his midsection, and brought his own weapon to the attack, a single, chopping blow with both hands on the sword grip.

The blow missed. Yngvar danced away. He was light-footed for such a big man, his bear trophies swinging from his belt.

Gauk knew better, but could not stop himself. He recognized his own foolhardiness even as he lunged after the seasoned berserker. He knew he should remain on the defensive — inexperienced as he was, he would have better luck parrying and giving ground than mounting an attack. And he should keep eye contact with his opponent, read the bigger man's intentions in his glance.

But he was being drawn into the fight, and sweat stung his eyes. A veteran sword fighter would have stopped, backed up a few steps, and wiped his brow. Gauk's blade flashed through the air, and he realized too late that he was unbalanced. The sword missed by an arm's length and plunged into the wet sand.

But Gauk was fast, too, and he wasted no time in recovering. He tugged his blade from the ground, and then warded off a series of blows, each one fiercer than the preceding, until the young man sprawled, his arms numb with the weight of Yngvar's assault.

The big berserker stepped back to give himself swinging room — a heavy weapon required striking distance. Gauk felt no surge of god-given power as he climbed to his feet, breathing hard. He experienced no transformation from young man to bear-like warrior, as he had in the past, and he no longer expected it. The god had chosen sides in this fight, and Gauk had lost. All that mattered now was preserving Hego's life. The young fighter dropped his weapon. He staggered forward, wrapped his arms around the larger man, and hung on.

Gauk grappled with the big berserker, pinning his sword arm. He struggled to hurl Yngvar to the sand, and nearly succeeded, lifting the heavier man off his feet. The big man grunted in Gauk's embrace, and the young man squeezed harder. Years of rowing and walrus hunting had made Gauk strong. If Odin would not help, then love for Hego and Hallgerd, for the brave village of Spjothof, would give Gauk the necessary heart.

He hugged Yngvar until the breath shuddered out of the berserker's body. He squeezed until Yngvar groaned. Something snapped in the barrel chest of this big man, cartilage or even a rib giving away. The berserker shuddered.

But he punished Gauk with the point of his bearded jaw, roaring, the big man's chin striking Gauk repeatedly until the young man's vision began to blur. *Odin, father of Thor,* prayed Gauk.

Save Hego.

Gauk must have lost full consciousness for an instant. When he was aware of what was happening, the big berserker was dragging him to the lapping waves, and flinging him down. Gasping with pain, grunting not like a bear but like a badly shaken man, Yngvar put a booted foot on Gauk's chest and cocked his sword arm, raising the blade high.

Gauk saw the blow approaching from an unexpected direction. There was nothing swift about it, and nothing skillful. Yngvar must have seen it coming, too. He looked up to see Head-Splitter held high. But the big berserker was too slow in blocking the ax with his sword, even though there was a long moment when Hego's weapon did not fall.

Yngvar gave a half-smile, as though still liking his own chances in this brawl. The salt suds at Gauk's ears hissed a loud and urgent communication. Odin's favor shifted from one man to another — *Gauk lives!*

Hego's ax split the big man's head.

Forty-one

Hego was freckled with bits of the berserker, and was moving slowly, cradling the ax in his arms. Gauk saw what had to be done. He gave a command, telling Hego to shove *Strider* off the shore, speaking right into his face, the way a steersman sometimes has to when his fellow seamen are stunned by a sudden squall. Hego moved toward the boat, but sluggishly, shoving the boat into the water and tumbling into her.

Gauk did his best to act the berserker. He seized his sword from the sand and gave out a roar, cutting great circles in the air. It wasn't real. It was make-believe — he was still only Gauk, apparently abandoned by Odin, and his right arm was tired.

But his snarling, frenzied display made the men on shore hesitate moments longer. Then, with a show of bravery, like men resigned to a desperate act, they resumed their attack.

They fought the way shield-carrying men so often do,

leading with their shields, shoving. Gauk grasped the edge of a shield and pulled the man down, hammering him hard with the butt of his sword.

The crowd closed around Gauk, so bunched together, they couldn't swing their weapons but could only jab, the points cutting his tunic, stabbing, missing. And not missing — he was hurt. His act, the rolling eyes, the bear-like roars seemed pale and fake to Gauk, nothing like the real surge of courage he no longer hoped for.

But these shorerakers were not as capable as they looked. They slipped and fell in the mess that had been the berserker. Gauk backed away, falling into the water, the salt stinging, the brine blooming red around him as he swam, one-handed. His sword was heavy — far too heavy. A threat to his safety now, it pulled his arm downward, anchoring his body.

Stones splashed around him — jagged cliff rubble, smooth shore stones, a rain of rocks hurled from the beach, distant figures running up and down the tide line collecting yet more missiles.

An oar dipped into the water close by.

Hego's big hand fell on his shoulder and seized the wool of Gauk's tunic. A smooth stone, as round as a barley cake, skipped across the water and struck Hego in the face. The young man gave out a gasp and released Gauk, and the young berserker once again felt his weapon dragging him downward.

He thrashed, kicking hard, and won another breath of air.

A few more strokes of the oars, another long reach, and this time Hego had Gauk in a mighty grip that dragged him from the salt sea and all the way into the boat.

They both realized too late that they had left it behind. The great, half-carved yellow thing on the beach beside Yngvar was the wheel of cheese.

Gauk was bleeding hard. He told himself that most of what ran off his body was salt water. He shivered, and let Hego row. The blade smith was good at it, and by the time the shoremen got their boats into the water and worked the oars through the oarlocks, shouting at each other, *Strider* left them far behind. The voices of the townsmen diminished, farther and farther away, until Hego reached the breeze of the open ocean.

Hego's eye was swelling shut. It was the same eye that had been injured in a fall, he explained, when he had called the crowded ale hall outside to watch a meteor shower many weeks ago. Far from a sense of self-pity, Hego sounded amused. The eye was determined to go through life swollen shut, he said, and until a medicine woman said the appropriate charm there was little anyone could do.

Hego used the forestay to lift the mast into position. Gauk moved cautiously, his wounds stiffening, and helped raise the mast with the leather ropes. Then, with the sail making the booming, cracking music that brought a shaky joy to his heart, he sank back.

Strider was taking on water. The sleek sailboat needed to be recaulked, her strakes sealed. Even the stoutest ship needed to be waterproofed, sometimes several times during a lengthy, storm-punished voyage.

Gauk fumbled for the bailer, a wooden scoop, and tried not to notice the bloody tint of the salt water he worked over the side.

Forty-two

Hego was chilled through, but he liked the feeling. He was very much alive.

The wind was with them, gale strong and cold. Hego kept a steady hand on the tiller, savoring the salt spray on his lips. From time to time he drank from the skin of Spjothof well water. Gauk rubbed saliva into his wounds and, like any fighting man, said they did not hurt.

They made the crossing from the land of Norway to the kingdom of the Danes in one night, following the route every Spjotman knew by heart. No traveler sailed with a chart or written list of ports, although Hego had heard that kings and tax collectors in distant lands kept such arcane items. Real seamen set their courses by lore alone, telling north and south by the habits of the waves around them, as remembered in way-poems and songs. Boats were rarely lost, although some journeys were easier than others.

Their passage was remarkably swift, but not unheard of.

In a gale blowing from the northwest, Errik No-Lip, a legendary boatman who had been scarred by frostbite, had sailed from Akerri to the land of the Franks in the same amount of time, but that was in the era of legends, when such feats were possible. Nevertheless, Hego took their own speedy sailing as proof that the gods favored their efforts.

Dawn sun climbed the sky. The water behind them boiled, the crests of waves stirred by the breeze. Hego could not see the horizon clearly, one eye closed tight again, and the other weeping from the salt waves that had swept the craft all night. Gauk trailed a fishhook on a line in the early morning, when the fish are hungriest, and snagged a large fish of a sort Hego had never seen before — surely another omen.

They ate the raw flesh gratefully, savoring even the innards. The food made them feel strong again. A protocol, unwritten and only half-understood, dictated their near silence on a day like this, battle behind them, and possible bloodshed yet to come. Hego would have to choose his words carefully, or he would offend the divine powers and cause ill luck.

Speaking sparingly, the two young men worked closer to the land as the sun climbed toward noon. Hego could make out the shapes of drift logs, whole trees, that bumped and groaned together in the easy swells.

*   *   *

Hego was concerned about his friend. All morning Gauk moved like a very old man. Sometimes he paused to flex his arms with a gasp.

Gauk caught Hego's expression of concern and laughed. "I'll have a few scars to show Astrid," he said.

Hego wondered if it would be appropriate to share his feelings now. "Do you think," he asked at last, "a death blow hurts?"

Instantly Hego hated himself for asking such a question, sure he would bring bad luck with his thoughtlessness.

But Gauk considered, licking his lips, blistered from the salt in the air. "Did the rock hurt you," he asked, "when it hit your eye?"

"Not at first," said Hego.

"So I don't think," said Gauk, "Yngvald lived long enough to feel the blow."

This reassured Hego. He did not like to think the big berserker had felt great pain. Hego wanted to think that the offensive, unruly berserker had left this life the way a drunken man leaves his senses: confused, muddled, and then at peace.

"You fought well," said Hego.

"No, I did not." Gauk grunted and, moving deliberately, he removed the bear pelt from over his shoulders and around his hips.

"You lured your attacker by pretending to be weak," Hego protested, disturbed by Gauk's show of humility. "Yngvar put on a brave show, but he was no match for you. You wore him out, so it was easy for Head-Splitter to live up to its name."

"You preserved my life," said Gauk, "and your own."

Hego laughed at this. When Gauk's saga was woven, Hego would count himself fortunate to be mentioned at all.

"The god took his favor away from me, Hego," said Gauk.

Hego did not like to hear the gods mentioned, except in song or prayer.

"Who knows what Odin will enable me to do," said Gauk, "against the Danes?"

"Oh, great deeds," Hego assured him uneasily.

How could Gauk explain to his old friend and neighbor that Odin had left an empty place in Gauk's heart, the way a bear leaves a footprint?

Against the Danes, Gauk feared, the two of them would be helpless. It was best, Gauk believed, not to weigh this thought too clearly, unless it become all too true. Hadn't Thor walked into the Ice King's cave and, challenged to show his prowess, wrestled with the cat of the world?

And Gauk still possessed sharp eyes, and a hunter's instinct. When he saw the vessels, and pointed them out, Hego squinted, startled. "I can't see them!"

"I see well enough," said Gauk. "Danish ships — they have red-striped sails and bright yellow markings."

Gauk helped Hego lower the mast, and the two of them lay side by side in the wet bottom of the boat. Drift logs, birch and spruce, lanced the tops of the swells, dangerous to a small boat like *Strider*, but excellent cover for the vessel, too.

Gauk peered over the side when *Strider* ascended a wave. It had been a while since he had seen warships, and he was astonished at how large they were, how the oars gleamed in the sunlight, beating in unison through the water.

The ships — three of them, with two more in the distance — crept along the coast as *Strider* bobbed among the swells. It was like the sorrowful poems recalling the search for missing comrades, the boats nosing every inlet.

"I can see them now," whispered Hego.

An archer, bow in hand, gazed out, in the direction of their hiding place.

The whispering water slowly leaked into the vessel. Hego let the sun warm him, and told himself he was not afraid of any Danish archer. Spjotfolk used arrows, too, sometimes. The Danes were cunning, but mere men, after all.

When Gauk assured him that Danish ships still coursed the far-off shoreline, Hego began to silently wonder what it would be like to grow old, full of stories, bright faces listening to his voice. Hego was confident, but not as self-assured as the heroes of sagas, who met every challenge with determination. Given a chance to slaughter a shipload of Danes, Hego would rather drift among the tree trunks like this, even the most dangerous logs, with bristling stumps where branches had torn free.

Hego could see more clearly now. Two mammoth drift trees closed in on the vessel. Each was still cloaked in moss, and a bark beetle scurried along the side of one of them. The great forest trees groaned against *Strider*. The vessel had been constructed by Njold the village shipwright for voyages in the ice, where drifting floes sometimes locked around a craft. The sailboat shivered along its length under the press of this drift timber, but she remained strong.

The Danish ships did not make the familiar sound of the ships Hego knew best. Something about the way the oarlocks were greased, and the sort of leather used in the rigging. And the songs the Danes sang as they worked, lilting tunes, bittersweet. A Dane spat, and the sound of it struck a log like a hand slap. Too close. They were drifting too close.

Hego huddled beside his friend, praying to Thor that, by sword or by sea, their deaths might be painless.

Forty-three

◈ ◈ ◈

All day, *Strider* took on water, the Danes rowing ahead, trying to avoid the tangled mat of floating logs. The Danish seamen shoved at the drift trees with oars, and rowed well away, searching the shore. Hego and Gauk took turns, bailing as silently as possible. Hego found that bark stripped from the trees, silently pressed into place, served to slow *Strider*'s leaks.

Then as the cool wind of late afternoon sharpened, the drift trees parted.

The Danes lifted sails and tacked seaward, each warship leaving long, foam-spinning wakes.

Gauk and Hego made short work of lifting sail and approaching the land, the surf along this low-lying coast weak and harmless, the seabirds giving way to broad-winged cranes, spearing the shallow water for fish.

They agreed that, while they were not lost, they did not know exactly where they were. The ancient way-poems told how to approach any port, by river marsh or open sea, including Gudmund's settlement.

> *Black sea, blue sea, past the stumps of trees,*
> *when the scent of marsh is strong,*
> *guide the steer-oar landward*
> *and the brackish tide is yours.*

Hego remembered the poem exactly that way, except for one detail. "Past the tall white stone," was the version he recalled. He sang it that way, and was met with Gauk's silence.

"Everything else you sang is correct," Hego added quickly, not wanting to hurt his friend's feelings.

"How can we see a 'tall white stone' from here?"

Hego was not sure how to explain such matters. "How could you see tree stumps?" he queried.

Night fell.

They smelled marshland — it was impossible to mistake sulfuric odor. Mud and decay, and that odd scent of fresh and salt water when they flowed together. They were close to their destination, as sea lore indicated, close to Gudmund's customary lands. But to be close to a destination was not enough, where sailing was involved. They needed to be certain.

Gauk steered the boat toward this faint but profound smell. Hego dipped his finger in the water, tasted it, and announced, "It's not as salty as the sea."

There were stories of a blind sailor who could navigate by tasting the water, reckoning by the saltiness whether a river flowed into the ocean, or a stream, or a sluggish marsh.

A tall white stone, some ancient boundary marker, did indeed loom against the shoreline, accompanied by the age-bleached stumps of what once must have been deep forest, long ago cut down.

The two young men ran the vessel into a bank of reeds, stiff rushes as tall as a man. A marsh bird complained and, in the starlight, started out across the wetland with its pulsing cry.

Hego heard the boat out in the waterway during the night.

A single paddle, in and out of the water, someone trying not to make a splash. The boater was good at it, but whoever it was could not keep the prow silent, the small boat parting the marsh.

Gauk drowsed.

Hego did not want to awaken him. He levered an oar into the water and stirred the mucky bottom enough to ease the vessel partway out into the dark. It was a mistake — the approaching sound stopped, the paddler alerted by the snapping of the reeds.

Gauk stirred and gripped his arm. "What are you doing?" he whispered.

Hego was clumsy at hurried explanations and merely shrugged.

The approaching craft was silent. The only sound was Hego's steering oar, cutting the water.

Gauk took up Whale-Biter.

"Can you see how many men there are?" asked Hego. He would die soon, he was convinced. But there was only one paddle out there on the water, Hego knew. One paddle, the person wielding it sitting perfectly still.

Even Hego could see what happened then — the sudden glow of a fire rising up over the marshland, distant rooflines reflected in the water. An alarm iron rang out, and distance-muted cries reached them.

A town was burning.

The solitary figure in midcurrent continued to say nothing, but there was a creak from the boat as the paddler turned, looking back toward the ascending blush of the fire.

Confused, Hego ran the key passages of the way-poem through his mind, trying to determine once again their exact location. There could be no mistake.

He said, "Freylief is burning."

"Gudmund's town is on fire!" agreed Gauk in a hoarse, excited whisper.

They peered across the fire-gilded marsh. How long could the lone paddler hold his breath? And who would be wending the marsh all alone in the dead of night?

Hego shivered, filled with hope. He leaned forward and licked his chapped lips, ready to make an experimental signal, the customary greeting of Spjotfolk in darkness.

Before Hego could make the signal, the message reached them through the damp night air, the same *click-click-click* the hawk owl makes to its young.

Hego cut a broad sweep with the steering oar, digging deep into the muddy bottom, propelling the boat forward. In their haste they failed to make the answering signal in return, and a woman's voice greeted them across the dark, an even-voiced, quiet fragment of the old song: *Under sky, above the sea / You will not take me alive.*

Hego stood, putting one hand to the mast to steady himself. He kept his voice as low as possible.

"Hallgerd?"

Forty-four

◈ ◈ ◈

When she heard a voice she leaned forward in the darkness. She fervently wished she had a seal spear, or a skinning knife — or even a sheep mallet. Any sort of weapon would be better than this oar.

Hallgerd had heard a human voice call her name in response to her signal. She was all but certain of this. The recent period of solitude, however, had made her mistrust her hearing. The mind could hear what it desperately wanted to — every child in Spjothof knew that. Now there was no sound in the marsh but the drip of muck from her oar, and a corresponding whisper somewhere ahead.

Another oar, out there across the marsh.

She recited a few phrases of a cherished courage-poem. The marsh was dimly illuminated by the shifting glow, Gudmund's town burning. Cries reached her from far off, and the steady iron stroke of the alarm pulsed through the dark. She felt a stirring of satisfaction for the damage she had set into motion, and at the same time a throb of sympathy for the ordinary folk of Freylief.

Let them learn, she thought, never to set foot in Spjothof.

Reeds crackled ahead of her, and a vessel parted a wall of vegetation. Hallgerd discerned two figures and the slender shape of a mast in the muted glow. A voice called her name again.

Her breath caught.

But it wasn't possible, surely. Could simple Hego have come all this way? A further consideration troubled her — how could he have survived his fight with the Danes? She dug her oar into the muddy bottom, and shoved the craft forward.

Hallgerd blinked tears of gratitude.

She had never felt more relief at the sight of two friends. The two young men were excited, too, and stammered a joyous, hurried tale. It was garbled but filled with praise for *Strider* and told of some great deed involving Gauk and a wheel of cheese.

For the moment she remained in her stolen vessel, the sides of the two boats touching. There was a protocol to questioning someone who had been lost — the rescuers traditionally inquired which neighbor the newly found would visit first, which favorite landmark had been most missed, and other such questions. It was important to determine that a spirit had not taken on the guise of a missing person.

But Hallgerd was the one with the questions. "Where are the others?" she asked.

"I hope it will not displease you," said Hego, remembering now to use formal speech in addressing the jarl's daughter, "that the two of us have come alone."

"Entirely alone?"

"Indeed," he responded, with what sounded like a touch of wounded pride.

Well, this was not perfect news, she had to admit. In truth, this was not what she had hoped at all, but she knew that the gods provided in surprising ways. She was reluctant to put her next question into words, but she forced herself. "Was my father still alive when you sailed?"

Gauk assured her that he had been breathing, and with the best of charms, Thor's hammer, pinned to his breast. "Our jarl is as strong as the tide," said the young hunter.

The question was painful, but she kept her voice steady as she asked, "Tell me, if you can — how badly hurt is he?"

"Our brave jarl suffered a wound," said Gauk, feeling in his voice, "to his head."

Anguish swept every thought from her mind. She boarded *Strider* and asked Hego to break up the craft she had stolen. Head-Splitter did its work quickly. It took three blows, and the simple Danish vessel gradually filled with water, firelight reflecting off the welling interior as the boat began to sink.

Heat from the distant blaze shivered the stars.

Hallgerd recounted her own story, briefly, already imagining how the story would sound when she had knit it into a poem.

"Let the Danes seek a bride from us again!" said Gauk when she concluded.

She ran her hands along the darkened vessel, making an inventory of their meager supplies. She ran her fingers over the thick pale fur. "Why is there a bear pelt in this boat?" she asked. And bear paws, she did not add, huge, black-clawed things, smelling faintly of death.

"Odin," said Hego, "has taken Gauk into his hand."

"Is this true, Gauk?"

The younger hunter did not respond.

Hallgerd's father had been broad-minded about berserkers and their unpredictable violence. Hallgerd herself was sorry to learn that Gauk had been lost to a life of divine savagery. But among the Danes, it had seemed, a berserker could dwell in a neighborly fashion. Perhaps Gauk himself would be so fortunate.

She began to express such reassurance, but Gauk lifted a hand, asking for her silence.

"Don't speak of it, please, Hallgerd," said Gauk at last.

He described briefly the death of his good friend Snorri, and added, simply, "Odin chose me — for a time."

"*Strider* is leaking," Hallgerd offered, quite willing to turn her attention to another matter. As she spoke the stolen boat beside them vanished entirely with an odd, almost human gurgle, leaving only a few floating splinters.

"She was leaking quite badly," said Hego, equally pleased to turn from uncanny matters. "She leaked like the waterfall beyond Ard, until Gauk and I recaulked her with tree bark."

"She is taking on water again, perhaps," suggested Hallgerd, as gently as possible.

"A little, just now," agreed Hego.

She took Gauk's hunting knife and cut tidy strips from her thrall-wool cloak. "You'll find butter on the bread in my satchel," she said. "Knead the stuff into this fabric."

The two young men seemed to recognize an echo of her father's gently commanding tone, and responded immediately. They fervently nibbled at some of the butter before they put it to the practical use of waterproofing their vessel, Hego's skilled hands making short work of it.

She made a brief examination of the vessel's mast and forestay. *Strider*'s sail had been woven by Gauk's mother and her friends, and Hallgerd was not surprised to see that no needle and thread would be needed to repair the sturdy fabric.

Hallgerd took the steering oar. It was gray dawn, with a

caul of smoke between them and the rising sun. She was troubled at Gauk's weakness. His wounds were deep and his voice feeble despite his relief at finding her. Hego was travel-worn, too, his lips chapped and his hands blistered, but both young men were excited, exclaiming fragments of poems and battle chants.

Her father had taught her that a jarl and his family had to be quicker in wisdom, and deeper in compassion, than any of their shipmates. She encouraged her two friends to rest.

"Oh, Hallgerd, how could we sleep now?" exclaimed Hego.

"I have rested in hiding," she explained reassuringly. "I've slept enough for twenty voyagers."

It was an old principle that sleeping companions eat and drink less, and awaken ready to take their turn on watch. As the south wind strengthened — the immortal gods be thanked! — she saw the sails of Danish ships far at sea, combing the swells for any sign of their escaped captive. And she saw new craft, their sails filling with wind, coursing seaward to give the warships details of the night's blaze.

She breathed a hope into the following wind, praying that it might take news of her to her father, and give him strength.

Forty-five

Hallgerd recognized the exact moment that the five Danish ships caught sight of *Strider,* all of them at once. With a surge of spray at each prow, each ship deftly ran out her oars and turned toward shore.

Strider's sail in the daylight, bright against the expanse of marshland, had caught their eyes. As fast as the sleek sailboat was, Hallgerd knew that by midday one of the faster warships would capture her again, and that surely Gauk and Hego would lose their lives.

But she had not anticipated *Strider*'s speed as she gained the open sea.

It should not have surprised her — the shipwrights of her village were well regarded in ports up and down the northern coast. The boat chased down gulls, and plunged from wave to wave, the passing foam a blur. Hallgerd's heart leaped at such rising momentum — surely they would sail into the sky!

Occasionally Hego would stir, groping reflexively for Head-Splitter, and she would give him a reassuring smile. Sometimes Gauk would lift his head, his hand on Whale-Biter, and she would tell him that all was well. It stirred her to pity to see how gratefully they welcomed sleep.

It was sweet sailing. All day *Strider* conquered the sea between the kingdom of Denmark and Norway, the booming south wind a blessing. The Danish ships persisted, however, falling into a long line in her wake.

Hallgerd could make out the painted white eyes of *Bison* in the lead, the ship seeming to stare across the distance, quickening Hallgerd's heartbeat. This sleek, proud vessel was swifter than the others, blessed with sleeker lines and a broader sail.

As the sunset approached, a great fatigue stole over her, even as she kept a firm grip on the steering oar, and she had a dream.

In her dream a ship swept up to *Strider*, crewed by silver-faced women.

A *snekkja*, a sleek, elegant warship, the craft kept away from the rocks and shoals that *Strider*, a lighter vessel, could sail over unharmed. Hallgerd was cold, her spirit stone. She did not want to look at these seafarers, but she kept turning back nonetheless to watch them going about the business of tightening riggings and bailing, like any sailing folk.

A man swung down, into the small boat, and the tiny *batr* crossed the empty water between them. The cloaked and hooded boatman spoke her name. And she recognized her father as he swept back the hood with one hand.

Rognvald made his way aboard *Strider*, and leaned over the slumbering forms of her two companions. He smiled as he realized they were fully lost to sleep. The wound in his head was grievous — she had to look away for an instant.

"Keep to the coast, Hallgerd," he said. "Follow the way-poems, as close to shore as you can." Her father smiled, tugged at the boat's rigging, and nodded when he found that the cordage was sound. He said, "Never let the surf catch you broadside."

He wore the silver amulet, Thor's hammer, pinned to his cloak, and his customary silver arm-ring. When he turned to depart he could not leave — she held him.

"No, Hallgerd," he said with a gentle laugh, "I have to go."

"Let them come for you," said Hallgerd.

"They will," he said simply.

"Let the spirits of death come here," she said, "and they'll see how a jarl's daughter can fight."

With that, she embraced him, and try as he might he was

too weak from his wound, and perhaps too loving to wrestle free. And *Strider,* even released from her steering grip, was faster than the *snekkja.* The women lifted sail, following the boat, her father laughing, gently protesting that Hallgerd was foolish. No one could outsail maidens from the Slain Hall.

Forty-six

When she woke, the Danish ships were closer, and the open sea gold and silver in the morning light. She believed that the dream had been a gift from some divine power, and that it warned her that her father was already drinking among the fallen heroes.

It was customary to share an important dream with one's companions, but she could not mention this extraordinary vision. Indeed, she fought hard to put the dream out of her mind. When Gauk saw how close the ships were now he made no remark, but drew Whale-Biter to his side. Hego did not spare them a glance. Anything they said or did might disturb the careful stitchery of fate and cause bad luck.

Hego offered her a last piece of Spjothof flatbread, and Gauk used an oilcloth on his spearhead, cleaning the blade, until Hego took over the task.

Already the drinking water was nearly gone, and what remained tasted salty as the goatskins became weathered and stiff. They took turns at the steering oar now, as Hallgerd's hands became blistered and cramped, but the well-balanced skip needed nothing more than their continuing prayers as it sliced the swells.

All day the Danish ships grew near. By nightfall the shore was close, with its white, rolling surf, and the ships had to stand well away from the rocks, backing oars at times, and shortening sails. *Strider* was able to thread the shoals, losing none of her speed, easily breasting the occasional submerged rocks.

The sheets, the leather ropes that worked the sail, were glazed with salt and sun, and had begun to fray — not at all like the stout rigging of her dream. The vessel's planks, although designed to be flexible, were working loose. Despite Hego's constant repairs, and his steady application of the bailing scoop, the interior of the boat was ankle-deep in cold brine.

But the Danish ships could not keep the pace. At last only *Bison* remained in the chase, the vessel's white eyes relentless in the darkness. White-haired Gudmund himself was easy to make out in the starlight, leaning over the ship's prow. And scarred Olaf, too, the man who had seized her and carried her from her father's house. To her heartfelt relief, Thrand was nowhere to be seen.

Bison grew so close she could hear the scraping of sea chests and creaking of leather as the Danes armed themselves.

Hego called out a song, his voice ragged. It was the chant of a mountain giant opposed by a Spjotman, the legendary villager Jom, armed with the ax of his great-grandfather. Unable to reach the giant's vitals, the Spjotman attacked the mountain creature's feet. It was a rousing song, one Hallgerd had always liked. Gauk brandished his spear and joined in the singing, his voice a rasp. Hallgerd, too, lifted her voice in the old poem in which the long-departed souls strengthened the hope of the living.

> *One and by one*
> *his ancestor's iron*
> *sings through the toes of the giant.*

The first Danish arrows lifted high through the stars, and fell just short, splashing in *Strider*'s wake. Gudmund stood near the archers, giving quiet directions.

The course *Bison* kept in the early morning light was cunning, parallel to the shoreline, veering wide of the boiling water wherever rocky shoals appeared. Hallgerd recalled well the storied skill of Gudmund's men, how well they could remember the soundings up and down the dangerous coast.

Arrows snapped at the sailboat, and when one clattered against the hull, another splashed ahead of her. Hallgerd took the steering oar from Gauk. She scented a change in the weather — the wind slackening, rain on its way. *Strider's* strakes squeaked, every peg in the sailboat complaining in the surf.

In the abating and sometimes contrary winds, the Danish warship was able to keep speed, while the smaller vessel tacked — sailing at an angle to the fitful wind — across *Bison's* course, and back again. Gauk and Hego worked the canvas and called fragments of ancient song to the Danes.

A spear ruptured the sail.

It happened without warning. One moment the canvas was full-bellied, the rigging taut in the renewed breeze. In the next a black spear glinted and punctured the full sail with a high-pitched, deafening *crack*. Then the shaft fell into the sloppy interior of the boat, leaving the iron head in the fabric.

The race was over, Hallgerd knew. Hope died in her. If they were within spear shot, they would soon be overrun. Hallgerd was heavy-hearted, but she would attempt to use her mental resources, and her skill in word craft, to spare her companions' lives.

She was not prepared for the squall of arrows.

A dozen shivered in the planks around her, several more hissing through the sudden screen of rain. One snapped through the air beside her head, and she sank into the safety of the hull. Hego was struck across his arm, and Gauk cried out as an arrow nipped him, the projectile glancing away into the wind.

All along Hallgerd had assumed that the very worst Gudmund would do was capture her again, and put her two shipmates to death at his leisure. But the steady onslaught of arrows indicated that the jarl was intent on vengeful butchery, immediate and complete. Arrows splashed and splintered, and another spear hissed through the rain, shattering against the mast.

Hallgerd searched her mind for some appropriate battle verse to chant while her heart's blood ran red.

When Gauk stood, swaying, clinging to the rigging, she thought the young berserker had suffered some sudden, agonizing wound. She cried out, and reached to support him when the brave young hunter fell.

But he remained there, his spear held high, as yet not seriously hurt. Gauk raised Whale-Biter, and gave voice to the sort of cry Hallgerd had heard described in legends, but had never heard in life. It was the bellow of a carnivore, a huge-boned, massive beast, far larger than any man.

That such a sound could be forged by Gauk's frame astonished the jarl's daughter. The approaching Danes leaned over the side of their ship, aimed their bows carefully, and sent arrows into Gauk's body as he rent the air with his roars, three arrows, four, finding his chest as he bellowed.

If I am nothing more than a fool, O God of Cunning, Gauk prayed, *I am nonetheless willing to die for my friends.*

Odin protect them.

Gauk hurled Whale-Biter high over the pursuing ship. The spear soared far above the mast top, over the fluttering weather flag above the sail, and vanished in the sea beyond.

Forty-seven

❖ ❖ ❖

The sunburned Danes, their eyes alight with anticipation, unceasingly mocked Gauk now as the young hunter slumped to the bottom of the boat. Hallgerd saw a certain heavy-footed logic behind their laughter as the shipload of armored Danes loomed over three travel-worn Spjotfolk. The all-but-lifeless young berserker's eyes weakly opened and shut against the falling rain, and Hego's song had died.

The wind strengthened behind them. Hallgerd felt the dimmest shiver beneath the keel as the sailboat grazed a shoal, but barely noticed the sensation as she prayed to the divine ones to spare the lives of her friends.

Then she felt a plan stir in her mind.

Hego knelt beside his fallen friend, his face ashen. Hallgerd kept her grip on the steering oar, piloting the craft through the boiling white water. She glanced back to gauge the Danish ship's approach, guiding the war craft closer to the rocks.

It happened in an instant. One moment the great, two-eyed ship was bearing down upon them. And in the next, *Bison* struck a submerged rock — one *Strider* had just grazed — with so much force the mast snapped, swaying sickeningly in place. The air was shattered by the sound of splitting timbers, the keel fracturing with a watery thunder. The heavy mast — with its sail and rigging and its twin spruce wood spars — crashed forward, crushing the archers in the prow of the ship, along with their white-haired chief.

It did not take long.

The warship's steerboard thrashed as seamen cried out in anguish. *Strider* skimmed the water ahead as the big ship unseamed on the boiling black rocks, strakes parting, broken keel rising up from the middle of the wreck. The big ship was in pieces. Graceful and flexible as the finest warships were, their planks were thin and, in a collision, no match for a jagged ridge of stone.

The armored men sank quickly, a few others crying out for help.

Hallgerd worked to bring the sailboat to, and turned her back toward the few desperate figures. She was satisfied at the havoc she had caused, but at the same time dismayed to see the humanity and the beautiful vessel so swiftly lost. Before *Strider* could alter her course, shields and sea chests careened in the seething water, and oars shattered into blond splinters on the rocks.

Olaf bobbed to the surface, supporting the bleeding, all but unrecognizable form of Gudmund. The white-haired war chief's mouth was agape, life streaming from his lips.

Olaf called out and waved, but after a long moment the two of them vanished beneath the sea.

Forty-eight

◆ ◆ ◆

Hallgerd leaned into the steering oar, the warm sun in her hair.

She had not always sat like this, two hands around the span of spruce. Earlier in her life she had been a jarl's daughter, without a solemn thought in her head, proud to be seen with her flowing tresses, looking out the window of her bed-chamber.

But that was centuries ago, in another life.

Seabirds played in a wide, ragged ring above. Hego recited the way-poem in his leathery voice, singing of the ancient route to safety.

> *Where the gulls spin*
> *and the white cliffs part,*
> *there your keel*
> *slices water home.*

Each plunge of Hego's bailing scoop pronounced the syllable *soon.*

"Look!" cried the young man when his song had drawn no response from her. He indicated the birds circling overhead. "We're almost home!"

Her smile was painful, her lips so badly blistered.

But it was true, as Hego had said. It could not be denied. The gulls were flying in a great, beautiful circle overhead.

And yet Hallgerd was afraid to hope, staving off what she knew would be disappointment, and even worse — inevitable grief. No apparition on the empty sea can be trusted. Who was to say this splash of bird lime on the cliffs was the storied entrance to the safe waters of Spjothof, and not a trick of the eyes?

Gauk was wrapped in his travel cloak, sword at his side, as was proper for a dead hero. But despite the final rituals, the farewells, and the promise from Gauk that he would bear their names proudly to the feast in the Slain Hall, the berserker did not quite die. A fever captured him, his unseeing gaze darting from mast to rigging to bare sky, and each breath was long and slow, but the final breath would not come.

Hallgerd had seen too many sick and injured folk to be able to believe that Gauk would survive. Trained by her mother in drawing arrows, she had extracted all but one, an arrowhead that snapped off as she worked it from his ribs. Hallgerd had bathed the young hunter's face with the very last drops of the drinking water, and Hego sang the oldest verses anyone in Spjothof could remember, the story of Thor resting his hammer in the mountains over his favorite village, blessing the place forever.

When the warships from home found them, that is how they were: Hallgerd at the steering oar, weariness blinding her to the golden light of late day, Hego in the prow, continuing in a low voice to sing the stories of hunters and warriors as he shoveled water over the side, and Gauk repeating whispered prayers with renewed strength.

It took her a long moment to realize what was happening.

Hallgerd saw the many prows parting white water, but did not trust what she was looking at. This was yet another fraud spun by petty divinities, in their jealousy of human hope.

Her name sang out from one ship, and another.

Raven of the Waves she recognized, and *Crane,* and behind those two warships the famous *Landwaster,* weather darkened. But she was puzzled at the other dream visions she beheld, hunting skips and freight boats, perhaps merchant *knarrs* from Ard, the lumbering, strong-timbered vessels outfitted with shields and spears.

Was it possible? she wondered. Had the lowly neighboring village joined in, too, proud and eager to stand with the Spjotmen against the Danes? Hallgerd knew this had to be a sun-pricked, full-fleshed illusion spun by an artful god.

The sailing army met *Strider* at the mouth of Spjotfjord, and from all around rang the chanting repetition of her name. A hallucination. A mockery, the gods teasing her before they stole her mind, dazzling her with phantoms in the guise of Astrid and Hrolf.

But when she set eyes on Lidsmod, she knew that he could only be real.

He was smiling and shouting something in the tumult — a bronze-skinned, sun-proofed Lidsmod, not the lad she had watched sail west earlier in the summer.

Gunnar was there, too, and white-crested Njord, and all the fighting men of Spjothof. If she was indeed among her friends — and there could be no doubt now that she was — a new fear filled her.

She could not bring herself to sound the question.

She took a few heartbeats to steady herself, mindful of her recent dream.

"Where is my father?" she called. Her voice was inaudible with the cheering, echoing chants of her name from cliff to cliff, and she had not been able to give the question any force, half-hoping the promised sad news could be delayed.

Now she wondered — was there a moment of hesitation in Lidsmod's features? Of course there was, she thought. There was a flicker of pain in all their eyes, surely. They had read the question on her lips, and they could not tell her the tidings.

Until an arm lifted, and a hood fell back.

The jarl himself leaned on Lidsmod's shoulder. The village chief was wan and weak, his head wrapped in white linen. He was calling out Hallgerd's name, his voice swept away in the great cheer that thundered. Oars were run in, dripping, the two ships closing together, closer.

And yet closer.

Her father reached across the narrowing gap.

Hallgerd stretched out her hand.